TRASH MOUNTAIN

JANE YOLEN

illustrations by
CHRIS MONROE

🍃 CAROLRHODA BOOKS
MINNEAPOLIS

Carolrhoda Books
A division of Lerner Publishing Group, Inc.
241 First Avenue North
Minneapolis, MN 55401 USA

Main Text set in Janson Text LT Std 12/18. Typeface provided by Adobe Systems.

For reading levels and more information, look up this title at www.lernerbooks.com.

Library of Congress Cataloging-in-Publication Data

Yolen, Jane.
    Trash Mountain / by Jane Yolen.
        pages   cm
    Summary: When the gray squirrels kill his parents, a young red squirrel vows revenge, finding unlikely allies in the rats and gulls of Trash Mountain.
        ISBN 978–1–4677–1234–7 (trade hard cover : alk. paper)
        ISBN 978-1-4677-7170-2 (EB pdf)
        [1. Red squirrels—Fiction. 2. Gray squirrel—Fiction.
3. Squirrels—Fiction. 4. Animals—Fiction. 5. Introduced animals—Fiction. 6. Survival—Fiction.] I. Title.
    PZ7.Y78Ts 2014
    [Fic]—dc23   2013030727

Manufactured in the United States of America
2 — BP —6/15/15

*T*his you should know:
Gray Squirrels are larger,
faster, and more aggressive
than Reds. They outeat the
Reds and outbreed them. They
are resistant to the Squirrel
pox that they alone carry. All
this scientists can tell us. But

Gray Squirrel
Sciurus carolinensis

they don't know if Grays are
smarter than Reds. At least
they don't know yet. But some
of us have our suspicions.

Red Squirrel
Sciurus vulgaris

The Old Fir Tree

Mother

Nutley

Father

Nutley lived with Mummy and Father in a dark fir tree way in the back part of Farmer Temple's garden. The fir was so old that it had bare branches halfway up its trunk. And halfway farther up, hidden behind the pine needles and pinecones, was a round hole. The hole was small but comfortable, with a soft bed of pine, feathers, and fur, and decorated with flowers and leaves of the season. Mummy made sure of that. When each season had gone by, she would mat down and shred the old stuff. Then out she would go to gather the new. It insulated the hole and kept the temperature perfect all year-round. Even in the grayest, coldest part of winter, the hole was warm. Even in the brightest, hottest part of the summer, the hole was cool. And this was how it should be, for after all, the hole was home.

Mummy and Father had never tried to live in the hazelnut trees on the sunnier side of the farmhouse, next to the lazy stream that ran along the front of the farmhouse. The stream ran over twenty-one stones before tailing off under a small stone bridge. In fact, Mummy and Father never even went near that small stand of trees. And yet, it seemed to Nutley that it made much more sense to live there, close to their favorite food—hazelnuts—and farther from fears of Fox and Owl, who preferred hanging about the farmyard, where mice and rabbits were easy pickings.

But whenever Nutley asked why—and he asked often—Mummy shook her head and Father explained: "To do so is to Court Disaster."

"Why Court? Why Disaster?" asked Nutley long before he had a chance to find out for himself.

Father didn't answer. Instead, he scratched at a pinecone in search of loose nuts, as if the pinecone was much more interesting than any question Nutley might pose.

"Never mind, dear, never mind," Mummy said. Then she recited,

> Beware Red Fox and Owl Light,
> Beware blood jaws and Owl Flight

before putting wet paws to Nutley's ear tufts, which both tickled and soothed. It also made him deaf for the moment, which successfully stopped any further conversation.

***

When he'd been younger and asking those sorts of questions frequently, Nutley always spoke while hugging his acorn doll or his crinkly grass pillow or his old bean rattle or some combination of the three. They lent him comfort in discomforting moments.

At those moments, Mummy and Father would smile at him and pet him and call him *sweetling* and *sunshine*, *dearling* and *son*. And sometimes they even answered his questions, though not in any way he really understood.

He was a bit spoiled, of course. He'd been the smallest of the litter, but his brothers and sisters had died of the pox one right after another. "In two weeks," Mummy said when feeling especially sad. So now he got all of his parents' attention. That was fine last year, when he'd been little and not able to bounce around and climb, not able to run in the sun or make it out to the bendy part of the smallest tree branches.

Now he was much too old for toys. The doll and the

rattle and the pillow lay discarded under his bedding in the hole. Discarded—but not entirely forgotten. Sometimes in his sleep, he would turn over and one of them would lump up under him and then—only half awake—he felt around for it. Hours later, when he woke fully, holding the doll or the pillow or the rattle, he would hastily rebury it under the bedding before anyone could see. He didn't want to appear childish. Not even to Mummy and Father.

Especially to Mummy and Father.

***

But now Nutley was old enough to know the answers. The full and true and real answers. He knew them but wanted to understand them as well. After all, he was growing, no longer a pup but a yearling. His tail and ear tufts had turned redder and occasionally fluffed properly. And real questions, longer questions, difficult questions seem to fluff into his head all the time.

"Why can't I run and play over in the sunny end of the garden?" he'd asked Mummy just the other day. "Why can't we pick up hazelnuts for winter instead of just the same old pine nuts?" he asked Father.

Actually, he thought he understood the answers already, but he wasn't absolutely certain. If only he could hear a true, full, real explanation from a grown-up. When a grown-up spoke about such things at length, those things usually became clear.

He chased his tail and fluffed his ears and waited to hear what they had to say.

But Mummy and Father only talked to him in short, sharp sentences, as if they were annoyed with him or thought him slow to understand. Or—and this was the most frightening thing of all—as if they didn't love him quite as much anymore. They certainly had stopped calling him *sweetling* and *sunshine*, though Father still called him *son*—but only when he was angry.

Nutley looked steadily at them both, his eyes dark and shiny as wet river pebbles. Father always said that one should look directly at the Squirrel addressed. And so Nutley did.

"After all," Nutley continued, "I think hazelnuts are yummier than pine nuts." He realized after saying the last bit that it was a mistake. He should have just stuck with questions. And, after all, he had only had a hazelnut once. By accident. When Mummy had found it amidst the leaves she'd gathered. So maybe that wasn't a big enough sample. Father always cautioned that one ought not to make wild guesses.

"Because of the Grays," Mummy said, her voice and tail tense. "They are not a sharing race." Then her tail twitched. *Go away, go away*, it semaphored.

Father nodded, adding, "An *introduced* race at that." His face was pinched as if he'd eaten something sour—a nut that had gotten frostbit or a berry gone bad.

Introduced, thought Nutley, turning it over in his head the way he turned over nuts in his paws before biting into the meat. *Introduced*. He looked up brightly, speaking directly to Father. "I could be introduced to the Grays. Maybe they would like me." But he knew the minute he said it aloud this was not what Father meant at all.

Father dropped the pinecone he was holding and stared at Nutley for a long moment without saying a word. Not even, *son*. Then he turned back to work extracting the pine nut.

"Never mind, never mind," Mummy told Nutley quickly. "You would not like the Grays." Her tail was now kinked and trembling over her head.

Nutley wasn't convinced. The Grays seemed to have all the fun. And they shared with one another all the time. He'd watched them for hours. They played Catch-as-Can and Pass the Bean and Hide the Bounty and even Raid the Bird Feeders. And best of all, they played Nut Keep Away, flinging a nut across a wide circle of Squirrels. Sometimes, when one Gray buried an acorn, another unburied it.

What can be more sharing than that? Nutley mused. *Or more fun?* Since his parents didn't seem to understand that, he wondered if they understood anything at all.

***

Day after day, as soft, moist spring turned to sultry, dry summer and wildflowers burst spontaneously into color in the green fields, Nutley watched the Grays from afar. Often he longed to join them, his tail waving like a flag. Occasionally he would lift a paw to them, but either they never noticed, or they were ignoring him.

Once one of the smallest of the Grays—Nutley heard a mother call him Groundling—looked furtively over his shoulder in Nutley's direction and raised a tentative paw in return. He seemed to smile. Before Nutley could call out or smile back or do anything at all, Groundling had been roundly cuffed about the ears by his mother for his effort. He ran off wailing into the tall grass. Nutley could see the flag of his gray tail kinking and unkinking by a stand of brambles, signaling his distress. When he finally composed himself, Groundling left the safety of the brambles, looking neither right nor left but especially not looking over to the fir where Nutley watched.

He never made eye contact with Nutley again.

"Why?" Nutley asked over and over, his questions growing as short as his parents' answers. "Why?"

But Mummy and Father had grown rather tired of answering and soon enough they stopped altogether, simply shrugging or saying, "Figure it out yourself, Nutley."

And he tried. Truly he tried.

He made lists in his head of everything he observed. One of the lists went like this:

Grays eat nuts.

Grays bury other nuts.

Grays look at the sky and say, "Tsk! Tsk! I think it might snow." (Though it was still summer and it rarely ever snowed before the winter skies had gone grayer than the Grays' own backs, so surely they must have known.)

The list went on.

Grays unbury nuts.

Grays eat nuts.

Grays throw acorns against the thickest trees.

He played out little scenes in his imagination where he rescued Groundling. One time it was from a large Cat with so many teeth that even in his make-believe, he didn't dare get close enough to count them. Another scene had him the only one who noticed a Fox approaching through the tall grass and Nutley's frantic chittering saved Groundling, who was eating fallen seeds in Farmer Temple's sunflower bed, all oblivious to Danger. A third—his favorite—was where he leaped up and pulled a screaming Groundling from the clutches of a silent predatory Owl. And after each one of these make-believe scenes, the Reds and Grays became fast friends and Nutley with his parents moved into the hazelnut copse where they lived alongside the Grays, happily ever after.

Nutley loved telling himself these little stories and could bring them up at any time in his mind, day or night, until they almost became memories. Still, he knew deep down that he had never been so heroic. He had never rescued anyone. The truth was, he was only a Red Squirrel and a small one at that.

***

As summer dragged on and many of the brightest flowers dropped, so did Nutley's ear tufts and tail. Or rather they drooped, which, he thought, was almost the same thing. There was nothing he could think of to explain why Grays and Reds could *not* be friends. At least nothing that made any sense. So he determined to simply hold out the Paw of Friendship to Groundling and his family and see what would happen. Though he guessed, in his heart of hearts, that nothing would happen at all.

And there he was terribly, horribly wrong.

This you should know:

An introduced species—also known

as an alien or a naturalized or

exotic species—is an animal or a

plant not native to a place. It has

been brought, either deliberately

or accidentally, to a new location,

often by humans but sometimes by

natural means like wind or flood
or simple expansion. Sometimes
these introduced species damage
their new ecosystem. Sometimes
they spread disease or disaster.
Father was right to fear the Grays.

The Paw of Friendship

It took Nutley a couple of days to get his courage up. Out by the Rosebay Willowherb, he practiced what he would say. What he would say changed from day to day. It even changed hour to hour.

At first he thought it best to start with this: "Hello. My name is Nutley, and I am a Red Squirrel." But then it occurred to him that they could easily see he was a Red, and that perhaps it was best not to point out differences but rather to remind them how they were all the same.

We are all Squirrels, he thought. *Not Foxes on the prowl or Owls on the wing.* That should count for a lot.

He practiced what he would say, beginning with, "Hi, brother Squirrels." But of course, some of them might be sisters, and he didn't want to offend anyone. So he changed the opening of his greeting to this: "My fellow Squirrels," which sounded rather too much like Father.

He thought about "Sweetlings," but that was too much like mother and just horribly inappropriate.

"Friends . . ." though the Grays weren't that. Yet.

He even thought about saying, "Hi, buddy!" And winking. But doing so made him shudder. And if *he* shuddered, he hated to think what it would do to the Grays.

Eventually, after a hundred more tries, he came up with, "Hello, I'm Nutley. And you are . . . ?"

He nodded to himself, standing up tall on his back legs and addressing a stately purple spear of Rosebay Willow-herb that was already magnificently in flower. Sticking out his right paw, he said it again. "Hello, I'm Nutley. And you are . . ."

Someone pounced on him from behind, with a victorious *tchirring* sound, pushing Nutley down on all fours.

"Wait!" he cried, "I'm extending the Paw of Friendship."

There was a loud rush of laughter all around.

"Grays friends with Reds?" a voice called out. "Don't be stupid."

Another voice, dark and angry, added, "Or any more stupid than you already are, talking to the flowers."

Then a third voice, high-pitched, possibly female, cried, "Push him this way, Groundling!" and Nutley was flung sharply to the right.

Thinking this was the start of some sort of game like Catch-as-Can, only rougher, Nutley rolled onto his shoulder gracefully—well, pretty gracefully for someone caught unawares. He was about to jump up and turn around to tag Groundling, when someone else grabbed his tail and gave it a vicious yank.

"Hey," Nutley cried, "Not fair."

"*Hey!*" they all mimicked. "*Not fair!*" their voices sour and whiny.

Nutley didn't think he'd sounded quite like that. He was about to say so, when they all piled on top, knocking the breath out of him. And when he could breathe again, he realized he'd been hoisted up over their heads. They were standing at the top edge of Long Hill.

Nutley looked out over the drop. His stomach took a dive. The drop was, as the name of the hill promised, a long way down.

"No!" he cried. "Stop!" But that
only excited the Grays even more.

Nutley guessed what would be coming
next and curled up in a little ball, his tail over his
back, neck, and head.

"Altogether now," the Grays chanted, "Sling him!
Fling him!" and then they threw him down over the
edge of Long Hill.

Long Hill was not only long; it was steep. Steep
enough so that in the winter, the Grays like to take
leaves and slide down the hill on them imitating Farmer
Temple's grandchildren. Cautious Nutley had never

dared do such a thing. Last winter he'd been too small, of course. But he'd watched the Grays gliding down, laughing and calling out to one another, seeming to have a wonderful time.

But gliding down on leaf sleds and rolling end over end after landing from a very great height were two different things. Especially since the Grays ran alongside Nutley, beating him with thorny sticks as he went rumbling and tumbling along. The thorns hurt, and so did the burrs that clung to his fur as he rolled head-over-tail-over-head down the hill.

He landed with a *thump* against a stump of a big old chestnut tree that Farmer

Temple had cut down the summer before. It bruised his back and left bits of bark in the soft places, but mostly what hurt was his pride.

As Nutley lay there, the Grays all clapped their paws together and someone cried out, "Cheers for Groundling!"

He heard footsteps as someone came up close to him.

"Is he done for?" came a shout.

The Gray who'd come near to him called back, "Probably." It was Groundling. He recognized the voice.

Nutley held his breath and tried to act dead. He didn't know what he would do if Groundling poked at him or tried to turn him over. Maybe jump up and run. Only where could he run to?

He waited and waited, holding his breath as long as he could, but there was no rustle of leaves, no sound of footsteps coming closer.

Nutley thought that Groundling must have gotten tired of looking at a dead Squirrel. Or maybe he just took pity on Nutley. Whichever it was, Nutley was not to know, but finally, he heard footsteps running away from him and Groundling's voice now far away, calling to his friends. And then shouting and laughing, the Grays raced away to play Catch-as-Can all the way back up the hill.

At last, Nutley let out a long breath and gulped in a new one. He stretched a little. Now he finally understood what Mummy had meant. The Grays were *not* a sharing race. Or at least they didn't share with Reds. And not a caring race, either. In fact, they were dreadfully mean. He lay on his back a long time beside the stump, trembling, and horribly afraid that the Grays might come back down and beat him some more.

He whimpered a bit but not too loudly and hoped nothing was broken. Or at least nothing important was broken. And he waited to get his breath back . . . if not his courage.

At last, standing up painfully, ear tufts drooping, he looked around.

No Grays at all.

He gave a huge sigh. Evidently with the Grays, it was out of sight, out of mind. At least that was *something* good he could say about them: they had a short attention span.

Nutley couldn't *see* the Grays any longer, but he could still *hear* them, raucous and rollicking on the other side of the hill. He stayed beside the stump until their voices faded away. Perhaps they'd gone off to the front garden or the hazelnut woods. Perhaps they'd gone to their own holes to sleep.

Then quietly trembling and hurting almost every-where on his body, Nutley limped back home.

***

"Was that a Disaster?" he asked Father when at last he'd made it to the fir tree.

Father was on the stump, working on cone cuttings. He looked at Nutley and nodded sadly but said nothing. Cone cutting was hard work.

"*Very* much a Disaster," Mummy told Nutley, holding his head between her paws and examining him all over but especially looking at his eyes and nose and ears for cuts and bruises. She washed his ear tufts with quick little licks. "*Tsk*," she said. And then, "Poor dear," as if she didn't like what she found. Afterward, she held him close.

Too close, Nutley thought, hoping nobody but family was watching. Her long fur got up his nose, and he began to sneeze.

Really, he thought, *I am all right. I am much too old for such cuddling.*

But Father was not so soft with him. "Grays are but a short step above the Lowlifes," he said. "One short step. You know they are an Introduced race." Harrumphing, he continued. "Fuzzy-tailed sewer

Rats, that's what they are. They eat . . ." and he said this final bit with disdain, "flower bulbs from Mrs. Temple's garden."

Nutley was aghast. *He* was never allowed to go near that garden. Farmer Temple had a shooting stick and was not loathe to use it. Great-Great Uncle Lucius had gone that way, back in the days before any Grays were around. There were rumors about Moles being shot at all the time. And the neighbor's big, black, one-eyed Tomcat had been killed by the shooting stick, though that, Father often said dourly, was no great loss at all.

"They're very Dangerous," Mummy added. "They carry diseases."

"The bulbs?" Nutley asked. "The shooting stick?" He had lost the thread of the conversation while thinking about Moles and the black Cat. And Great-Great Uncle Lucius.

Father rolled his eyes.

"The *Grays*," Mummy explained. "Try to keep up, dear."

She fussed over him a bit more until he got quite tired of it and pulled away from her. Instead, he went up onto a small, swaying branch at the very tip-top of the tree. It was too small for either Mummy or Father. There he perched and watched the Grays playing in the hazelnut trees and running along the rooflines of

29

Farmer Temple's sheds on their way to raid the bird feeder. They had doubtless already forgotten about him, but not Nutley. How could he forget? He ached everywhere, and his hurt pride still prickled.

The Paw of Friendship, he thought, was a very bad idea indeed.

Well, actually Nutley wasn't thinking a lot about the Paw of Friendship. Not really. Really, he was thinking that *Dangerous* must be a desirable state. After all, he himself wasn't Dangerous. Reds were never Dangerous. Trying to do something nice, like offering the Paw of Friendship to an enemy, had backfired. Look where that had gotten him! Pummeled and pounded and sore.

So, he thought, *maybe being Dangerous is more valuable than being nice or being a friend.* Certainly the Grays had come a long way with danger at their core.

***

That very day, though he still ached from the beating with the thorny sticks and he hadn't quite gotten rid of all the burrs he'd picked up rolling down the big hill, Nutley started practicing being Dangerous. He bared his teeth, twitched his tail, and opened his eyes so wide they looked big and fierce as if fire were shooting from them. He even learned how to growl deep in his throat.

He'd show the Grays what being Dangerous really was.

He'd show them all.

Below on their larger branches, Mummy and Father watched him. Mummy clapped her paws once or twice. Father didn't look quite so amused.

But Nutley?

Despite the aches and despite the pains, Nutley felt wonderful.

This you should know:
Red Squirrels mostly eat
the seeds of trees, stripping
conifer cones to get at the pine
nuts. They also eat fungi; bark;
flowers; berries; young shoots;
and when they can get them,
hazelnuts. Unlike the Grays,
Reds do not eat acorns. And
they are not a Dangerous race.

Attack

Nutley continued to practice baring, twitching, and growling whenever he could, and by the end of three weeks, he'd gotten quite good at all three. However, he'd had to give up the widening of eyes.

As he explained to Mummy, "It just gives me a headache."

"Of course it does, dear." She patted him on the head and went back to decorating the hole with the first red leaves of fall.

Nutley shrugged. "I'm off then. As promised."

Father didn't say anything, just harummphed loudly and looked entirely discomforted. But it was no worse than he'd done for days.

Nutley went out of the hole, refusing to look either right or left for Danger. After all, how could he show fear? Anyone truly Dangerous instills fear in others. So without checking for possible peril, he raced off to glean seeds in the far field where Farmer Temple had planted corn and sunflowers. Nutley did it because in one of his more sharing moments, Father had said he was *so* tired of pine nuts and bark, and Mummy had pleaded for something—*anything*—other than mushrooms. Full of Dangerous Thoughts, Nutley had volunteered to go out at first light to find them sunflower seeds, though he'd never been to the far field all by himself before.

The rising sun stained the sky as bright as blood. Because the early harvest was over, the corn had all been cut down yet the cornfield wore its stubble manfully. As Nutley got closer, he could see several rows of huge sunflowers that were still standing, their large yellow faces turned toward him. A few sunflowers had their heads bowed, but the rest gazed straight ahead seemingly unworried about the future.

Like me, he thought, baring his teeth at them. *Dangerous.*

He went up and down the rows, finding little enough that Mummy and Father could eat. There was a bit of cob here, some dry and wizened kernels there, but they were not really edible. A small breeze danced along between the rows and ruffled his ear tufts. In the little round garden of sunflowers, he found a few fallen seeds that were plump and inviting. Those he stuffed into his cheeks. Then he sat down to contemplate his next move, enjoying the warm sun on his back.

Nothing better, Nutley thought, *than being Dangerous and in the warm sunlight.*

Suddenly he heard distant screams.

Screams? He looked around. This far from a tree—any tree—put him in Danger. And while he had practiced being Dangerous, he knew there was no fooling around with *real* Danger. Like Foxes. Like Owls.

Quickly, he raced up the row to the end of the field farthest from the farmhouse. The cries were louder here, but he couldn't quite make out who was crying

or why because there was such terror in the voice. His tail twitched, signaling its go-away sign.

Now he heard a whole range of cruel and awful chittering laughter, high and unrelenting. It was the laughter—not the cries—that made his skin crawl and the hairs on his tail stand straight out. He got up on his hind legs and stared fearfully toward the sound. Squirrels are not terribly farsighted, so all he saw was a blur.

Remembering that he was now Dangerous—or at least he could make a good imitation of it—Nutley bared his teeth and growled. He twitched his tail. He thought: *Nutley to the rescue!*

He said it aloud. "Nutley—to the rescue."

His feet tried to respond, though for a long moment they didn't move.

He said again, even louder, "Nutley to the rescue!"

This time his feet listened. He started over circling to the west, skirting the fir tree, and hid at last in the tall grass beneath the shadow of the Long Hill.

At the hill's bottom—where not three weeks earlier he'd crouched bruised and trembling—he suddenly recognized the screamer. It was Mummy, only he hadn't realized it was Mummy before because her terror had been so great that it made her voice high and shaky.

Now he forgot all about being Dangerous and

simply raced up to the top of the hill where he saw with astonishment—and then with growing horror—that the Grays were mounting a full-scale attack on his parents' fir tree home. He'd never heard of such a thing.

He wanted to race to their aid at once. He wanted to push a closed, Dangerous paw into the face of every Gray he could find. But deep down, he knew it would do no good. Reds are simply smaller than Grays. Weaker. If he went now, he could be terribly hurt. He might even die. And then Mummy would be unhappy and say "Tsk" again. Father would scold and look disappointed.

And if he died, his parents would never get over it. Their last pup.

But he couldn't stop himself from inching forward one paw at a time till he was almost within range of the tree. He was very quiet and made no sound. The grass barely moved. He wasn't Dangerous, but he was Stealthy. Stealthy is Healthy, Father always said.

Suddenly the Grays ended their raid and passed close to where he crouched, trembling, in the tall grass. They headed back to the hazelnut copse. Some even passed right by his hiding place as they ran, so fast they didn't even notice him. Groundling was in the lead.

Nutley waited until they were far, far away, tremors running up and down his back. When the Grays were out of sight, Nutley crept back to the bottom of the hill so as not to be seen should any of them turn around. He thought he would wait only a few minutes. But somehow, he couldn't get his legs to carry him up the hill. Terror and the trembles can defeat good intentions every time.

**

In fact, Nutley waited until late afternoon, eating three of the sunflower seeds, waiting till clouds settled over the sun, which made the day seem even darker. Only then did he feel brave enough to creep home, circling around and coming to the tree from behind. so none of the Grays still celebrating near the farmhouse night spy him. He hoped that the local Crows—such nosy, noisy, annoying Birds—would not give him away.

Things with Wings, Father always said, *are not to be trusted.* And knowing what he did about Owls and Hawks—both hideous Squirrel killers—Nutley had to agree.

"Mummy," he called when he got near, his voice muffled by the seeds left in his cheeks. "Father."

Unaccountably, they were both silent.

Maybe, Nutley thought, *maybe they have gotten tired of waiting for me and gone to the field to find food themselves.*

He climbed up the back of the tree and only at the last, when he was hidden by the pine needles, did he sneak into the hole.

Mummy and Father were not there.

Scrambling to the end of his favorite branch—the bendy one—he looked out toward the field. But it was too far away and blurry for him to make out anything as small as a Red Squirrel and he could see no movement at all, except for a Hawk making lazy circles in the sky. Father would have already seen such a killer and made sure he and Mummy were hidden. Nutley was certain of that.

He started to back down the bendy branch, looking left and right. By accident, he looked straight down and saw—*oh, horror!*—both Mummy and Father lying broken and still at the bottom of the tree.

Nutley scarcely dared to pause long enough to shed a tear, knowing that speed was now of the essence. First, he went back into the hole, grabbing up what possessions he could stuff in his cheeks on top of the few seeds that were already there: his acorn doll, his crinkly grass pillow, and his old bean rattle.

Then, speeding down the tree, he stepped onto the ground where pine needles lay thick and soft all around. He stopped for a moment and touched Mummy's paw. It was stiff and cold. Father lay on

his back, his legs splayed out in uncharacteristic abandon. Nutley realized that they had been long dead. Maybe for hours.

"I've killed them," he whispered, thinking that he might have helped if he hadn't been cowering while they'd been fighting the marauding Grays. But he knew in his deepest heart that he could not have saved them even he'd tried. That didn't make him feel any better. If anything, it made him feel worse. Worse because he hadn't tried. He'd only hid. Hid and nibbled on a seed. Or two. Or three. And what was Dangerous about that? *Nothing at all.*

Nutley could hear the Grays singing songs somewhere in the distance, drunk as the local badgers—on elderberries probably. He shivered. He had to leave, leave now, and never come back. Leave his Mummy and Father and the little fir tree, the only home he'd ever known.

He took a moment to gather up pawsful of pine needles and sprinkle them over his parents. There was nothing more he could do for them. Nothing except all he really wanted to do was to weep and scream, scream and weep. Or maybe to race over and attack the rioting Grays. He even thought briefly of falling honorably in battle.

But he was too like Father. He could think things through when he had to. He knew he had no time for any of that Dangerous and Honorable stuff now. His cheeks were too full to even whisper a curse at the Grays, but his thoughts were dark and bleak. He looked down again at Mummy and Father all covered with the pine needles.

Good-bye, he thought, miserably. *I love you.*

Then he dashed back behind the tree, went over to the shadow of Long Hill, and made his way across the tall grass due west towards the Winding Road, careful to keep the sheds between himself and the sound of the squirrels making fools of themselves at the farm. He guessed they were in the hazelnut trees. But he knew he had to go quickly. He was running out of time.

***

Nutley knew he had to take care, since he had to make sure that there were no Cats about. Or that the Red Fox that Father always warned of was not on the prowl. He hoped the Hawk had gone. He also worried about Owls, of course, and shivered thinking how fierce and silent they were. But it was still day and he had time before Owl Light and Owl Flight, so he kept on running.

He came at last to the Winding Road. He didn't

know which way to go. He only knew he had to go far away from the fir tree, far away from the familiar dirt paths of the Temple farm.

Stopping, he stepped gingerly onto the hard, gray surface, a place he'd never set foot on before. It felt strange and unyielding, not like the grass or soil of the farm, not even like the gravel of Farmer Temple's driveway. For a moment he stood trembling, nervously shifting the few possessions packed in his cheeks.

What to do? he thought. *Which way to go?* As he stood there, dithering, some of the Grays spotted him from the deck rail.

"Hey, lookit there!" one cried.

"Is that our Red or some blood splotch on the road?" another yelled.

"If not now, he soon will be. One small flattened fauna!" shouted a third. Nutley thought it sounded like Groundling.

There was a loud chittering. Though Nutley listened with all his might, he couldn't really make out how many of them there were or, indeed, where they were. He suddenly feared they'd perched atop the three sheds. He knew he didn't dare stay a moment longer and began to run along the macadam, choosing a direction without thinking, sudden fear helping him put on a burst of speed. The hard road sent sharp pains up his legs and into his belly. Way behind him, maybe even back on the porch railing, the Grays continued to jeer.

"Go along, ye small weenie!"

And another—it might have been Groundling—added, in a high-pitched voice: "He's naught but a doomed member of a doomed race."

Then they all laughed.

For the first time, Nutley believed them. Doom settled on his slim, red shoulders and weighed him down, which made running even harder. It was like swimming in the Long River, something that a Squirrel never did. *Or would never want to do,* Father always said, there being Squeals in the water, long snaky things with big jaws that would like nothing better than a meal of Squirrel.

And then Nutley remembered. *Father! Mummy!* In his mind, he immediately conjured up how they had looked, so stiff and silent and cold covered only by a few pawfuls of pine needles, which did nothing to disguise their deaths.

Only then did the tears finally began to fall, which made navigation on the Winding Road a bit haphazard, but he didn't dare stop to wipe the tears away.

This you should know:

Not far from the green trees and the long green meadow, around a deep bend in the Winding Road, sat Trash Mountain, only no Squirrel of character ever dared go there. It was said that any nuts on Trash Mountain came wrapped in plastic bags. It was said that the very earth of Trash Mountain was sullied and malodorous,

which is another way of saying it
stank. Besides, the mountain was
only frequented by Rats and Gulls
and other Lowlifes. Could a Red find
enough food on Trash Mountain?
Only Rats and Gulls and other
Lowlifes knew for sure.

Into the Trash

It was getting dark by the time Nutley came to the first curve on the Winding Road. Dark meant Owl Light. He knew he needed to find a hole for the night and soon.

Suddenly he saw two great lights hurtling toward him, even brighter than the lamps in Farmer Temple's back room. Indeed, he'd seen such lights before but always from the safety of the fir tree. However, Father had told him all about them. How they were always attached to a large People Carrier. How they hauled death in their souls. This one was black, like a moving hole, and careening from side to side on the road.

Desperate to avoid being hit, Nutley sprang to the left, opened his mouth, and screamed. He hadn't meant to, but all of the awful day suddenly flooded over him. As he screamed, everything in his cheeks spilled out onto the road behind him—seeds, doll, pillow, rattle—where they were immediately crushed under the large, round things on the underside of the Carrier. In fact, Nutley himself was almost crushed with them.

"Oh, no!" he cried but didn't take a second longer to consider the loss of his precious possessions, for now they were the consistency of sand. Useless. Worthless. And Flat. As he would have been had he not jumped away at the last possible second, off to the side of the road. He could see the Carrier turning around and inexplicably coming back toward him. Sometimes People were impossible to understand. No—*most* of the time they were.

Now in a great panic, Nutley headed off to the left along a smaller spur road that for the moment seemed the only safe route till he realized a carrier could there, too. A guard house and a wire fence stood on his left. He slipped through one of its many small holes that were just the right size for a Red Squirrel. Briefly, he wondered who had built it that way and sent out a small prayer of thanks.

The Carrier's lights moved backward and then were replaced by two red lights that soon disappeared along the Winding Road.

Nutley couldn't take the chance that the People Carrier would return again. Father had told him many a story about animals crushed on the Winding Road, flattened like Great Aunt Cornelia, whom he'd never known, left for the Things with Wings to devour. Shuddering, he ran even farther away from the fence, though he could still feel its cold metal presence behind him.

Before he knew it, he was knee-deep in thick, horrible garbage, and that—for a Squirrel—is very deep indeed.

"Trash Mountain," he whispered. Now that his cheeks were empty, he could speak again. He said the name once more, this time with an audible tremor. "Trash Mountain." That had to be where he was.

He must have come to Trash Mountain from the side. He'd heard the stories: *Here be Rats as big as Collie Dogs. Centipedes that sting. Slugs fast enough to steal a Squirrel's nuts.* He shivered and looked around frantically for an escape. But behind him he thought he could still hear the jeering Grays and the grinding sound of the People Carrier coming back for a third try at crushing him.

Probably just my imagination, he thought. But the thought was not comforting.

He didn't dare chance going out to the Winding Road again. Besides, he knew there was nowhere else for him to go. At least the Grays wouldn't follow him here. They knew the stories as well as he did. And unlike him, they didn't need to escape into this awful place. He couldn't guess what the Carrier would do or the People.

"Mummy..." His lower lip trembled. "Father..." He squared his shoulders, then—bearing the unbearable—he marched even deeper into the trash.

***

The smells. Mummy had never mentioned the smells. Nor had Father. The smells coming from Trash Mountain were rich, potent, moving, even... *Enticing.* He wondered how low he'd already fallen to consider that. The smells reminded Nutley a bit of Farmer Temple's compost heap, which in the summer— under a long sun—was almost irresistible. Only these smells were a thousand times stronger. There were so many strands—sweet, sour, bitter, sharp, tangy, spicy, gamey, flowery, vinegary, and the pungencyof pine resin—oh, he couldn't name them all. They were simply overwhelming. He almost swooned.

"There, lad, don't be faintin' like an old lady." The voice had a bit of an edge to it and a lot of hidden laughter.

Nutley pulled himself together, turned, and saw on top of a hillock of garbage a large, fat, gray, and seriously ugly Mouse. No—no, not a Mouse, rather a bigger creature, with a longer, hairless tail. An elongated snout. And huge front teeth.

"Why—you're a Rat!" Nutley blurted. He'd heard of them, though he'd never seen one before. Farmer Temple's wife ran a clean home that housed several resident Cats.

"Not just a Rat. A Hanover Rat, a Norway Rat, or a Wharf Rat. Take your pick, bud. You were maybe expecting the Queen?" The Rat spoke while using his long tail to poke something green and slimy from between his teeth. He picked it out with one rather dirty paw. Popping the green back into his now-gaping mouth and swallowing, he let out a huge belch. He followed that with a strange whinnying laugh. "The *Queen*," he repeated, enjoying his own joke.

Nutley didn't answer that. Mummy was especially fond of the Queen and even had a picture of her, torn from an old *Royalty* magazine, up on the wall of their hole. Besides, Nutley was careful not to tell the Rat what Mummy always said about *his* entire race. She called them "Common Rats." Telling the Rat that wouldn't have been polite. And possibly not safe, either.

"Now, lad," the Rat announced, "here you've come to Trash Mountain." He laughed again. This time it was a series of descending wheezes. "I'm what you might call the welcoming committee. Name's Naw. Nothing's silent." Another laugh, this one short and sharp, rather like the tap of a Woodpecker on a metal gutter.

Nutley didn't feel very welcome. And he certainly didn't understand Naw's humor, but that too wouldn't have been polite to say. Instead, he bobbed his head. "Pleased to meet you, sir." It was a sentence so filled with half-truths and outright lies that he felt sick to his stomach. And this on a day when there had already been much to feel ill about.

"I'm sure." The Rat grinned, which showed even more of the green stuff between his teeth.

For a moment they were both silent, and then overhead there was a loud concatenation: screams and cawings and the heavy flapping of wings.

"Gulls," said Naw. "I don't pay 'em no mind. And you shouldn't neither."

"Oh, I won't." Nutley spoke with rather more passion than was called for, but he was so relieved that there was someone to tell him what to do, now that Father was gone. "I won't neither." That last, ungrammatical though it was, issued forth almost as a sigh. He knew Father would have been appalled.

Naw grinned again, that disconcerting smile, part yellow teeth, part green stuff. "Now I'll show you The Ropes."

The Ropes? Nutley wondered for a long minute what the Rat could mean by that and why he needed to see these Ropes. In his experience, Ropes were used to tie things up and tie things down, not necessarily for the good. Like birdseed covers and feeders and cages. He almost shivered. But quickly—and eventually—as Naw took him up and down the runnels and channels, the tunnels and gullies of Trash Mountain, he learned that *The Ropes* was just a Rat phrase for showing someone around.

"That there . . ." Naw said, his paw making a circular motion around them, which included a rather ripe and inviting hillock of trash, "is off-limits to anyone but Rats."

Nutley noted the plural. "There are more of you?"

Naw put his head to one side as if considering how stupid one small Squirrel could be. Then he nodded. "There's Nawmer, my lovely bride. And our nine bouncing children: Nawman, Nawmal, Nawsome,

Nawmus, Naway, Nawgahyde, Nawtickle, Nawty, and baby Nawshus." His tail twitched with each name. He smiled, which did not improve his looks. "And nothing's silent in a one of 'em."

This time, Nutley thought he understood the Rat. But then again, perhaps not. *It's better not to presume when talking to lower orders*, Father always advised. To which Mummy had usually added, *Sometimes the Queen or her children go out in disguise.* Though it was hard to see how a Rat might be a Royal, in disguise or out of one.

But then he remembered—the Rat did say he was a Hanover Rat. And Hanover, Mummy had often said, was one of the Royal Houses of Britain and the Continent. *Better safe than embarrassed*, Father often warned.

"Okay," Nutley said, though he was really not okay with that many Rats in the neighborhood. Suddenly, the Rats' hillock was no longer very inviting.

"That one there's for the Gulls..." Naw said, pointing to an ocean of garbage that undulated at the foot of the hillock and ran for about two acres north.

"Absolutely," said Nutley. He didn't need to deal with Things with Wings. And especially not Gulls. Mummy called them *Garbage Collectors* and *Flying Rats*, and he'd often seen them in the big field following Farmer Temple's tractor or harrow, picking up anything the sharp knives turned over in the soil.

"And the rest is Open Territory, meaning . . ." Naw suddenly sat down and scratched behind his left ear, an action that left him incapable of speech for some time during which Nutley looked around and wondered what it *did* mean.

Naw suddenly stood up again, whatever itch that needed scratching now done. "Meaning . . ." he said, as if he'd never stopped in midsentence, "that you can fuddle around there."

Fuddle. It was an interesting word, and Nutley tried it out, rolling it around in his mouth as if it were a sunflower seed. He almost missed what was said next.

"And that . . ." Naw pointed to the sky where a giant tower of garbage teetered. "That's the *real* Trash Mountain, and it's off-limits to everyone."

There was a large White Box sitting at the very top of the teetering tower of trash. It had a door with a round window that opened and closed in the wind.

"Why?" Nutley asked.

"Why what?" Naw's left eye seemed to bore into him. It was a bloodshot eye.

"Why is it off-limits to everybody?" Nutley felt suddenly warm all over as if he had come upon the most important piece of information in the universe. The one thing that might help him regain his home and avenge his parents' death. *That* kind of information. "Is it Dangerous?"

Naw shook his head slowly from side to side. "Don't know. Just has always been—off-limits. To Everyone." He took a deep breath and added all at once, "Especially the White Box." He drew in a ragged breath, and when he expelled it, he said all in a single gasp, "Thosethatgoesindon'tcomeoutagain."

"Goes in where?" Nutley asked. "Comes out where?"

But clearly the tour of The Ropes was over, and so was Naw's interest in Nutley, because the Rat turned around three times as if chasing his long, hairless tail, then disappeared into a hole in the hillock. As it was the Rats' hillock, Nutley didn't follow. Having lived all his life knowing where the limits were—as defined by his Father and Mummy and the Grays—he followed his nose to the fuddling place instead and began to look for something to eat.

Maybe, he thought, *that's what "fuddling" means. Digging around for food.* He was delighted—even proud—of this insight and grinned for the first time since coming to Trash Mountain. Though thinking about food made him suddenly and overwhelmingly ravenous, which was Mummy's favorite word for being extra hungry.

This you should know:

Trash Mountain is over two

dozen acres wide and almost two

dozen acres long. It is completely

surrounded by a wire fence. There

used to be a Human guard there

every day of the workweek, plus

the third Saturday of the month. But

times being hard, the town had to cut

back on his hours more and more,

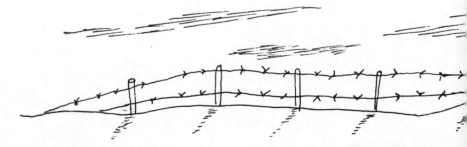

until at last the guard was only at
work on Saturdays nine to noon
and only in the new part of the
town tip, near the recycling area,
which is why there is no guard at
Trash Mountain during this story.
If there had been, things might
have gone very differently.

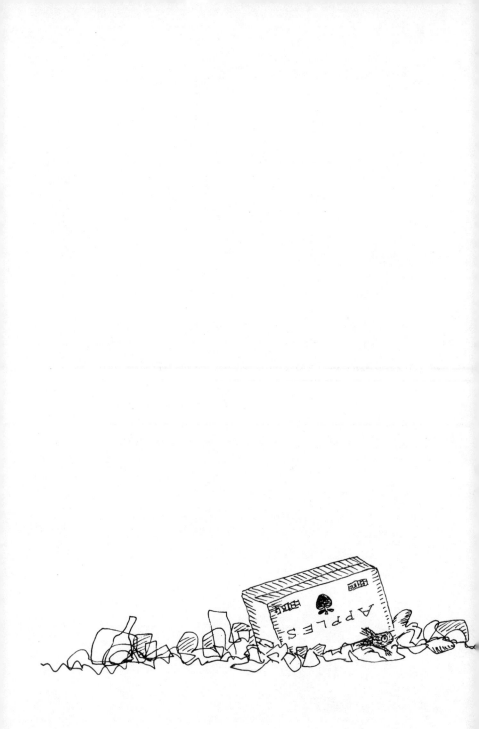

A Cry in the Night

Nutley found a couple of slices of greenish bread buried down amongst some rattling papers. The green gave the bread a kind of tang that he both liked and hated in equal measure, but at least it was food. There were several crinkly packets that smelled of nuts but were empty. He tried licking the nut smell, but that wasn't very satisfactory at all. He found three tins with gray stuff in them, but after a single sniff of each, he threw them over his shoulder toward the Rats' territory.

Better safe than sorry, as Mummy used to say. Or was that Father? He was already beginning to forget. He hated that.

Finally, by digging straight down, he discovered a treasure trove: three old hazelnuts. Nutley did a little happy dance, his tail bobbing up and down with delight. He weighed the hazelnuts carefully in his paws one at a time. Two of them were clearly full. He opened the third anyway, but it was only an empty shell—as he knew it would be. He scolded himself for the waste of energy and time. As Father always said, *Don't spend what you can't spare.*

By now Nutley's entire body was making a mumbling, rumbling sound. The two hazelnuts had only encouraged his tummy, not satisfied it. Mummy would have told him what he could and could not eat, and Father would have told him where to find it, but they were gone and he had to accept that. He was on his own. Not a comfortable place to be, but there it was.

Nutley began scrambling in shorter and shorter jumps around the fuddling place. There was no more food anywhere or at least nothing that wasn't gray, foul-smelling, or covered with little white crawly things that made a shiver go up and down Nutley's back.

Tired, exhausted, he was about to lie down in

the trash—*Which is where I deserve to be,* he thought miserably, *the Grays were right.* But his right paw felt something odd, stiff, and interesting. And when he'd dug it up, he saw that it was an overturned wooden box. The bad news was that the box was empty of anything resembling food. But when he cocked his head to one side and looked at it with a bit of imagination, Nutley realized that the box was very like a hole. Not a round hole in a tree but a hole nonetheless. He figured it could keep him safe from the night fliers, especially Owls, and so he turned it upside down; crawled in under it; and immediately fell into a deep sleep full of dark, disturbing dreams.

In one of his dreams, Nutley heard a cry. The cries were from his mother and father as they were thrown from the fir tree. And the sound of their hitting the ground was like the loud *bang-bangs* of the rockets Farmer Temple's grandchildren set off on holiday visits.

In another dream, his parents did not fall, but—like Flying Squirrels—glided soundlessly down and down and down. His father had often told Nutley tales about that exotic race, and maybe some of the stories were actually true. *How will I ever know now?* Nutley asked himself in the dream.

In yet another dream, he ran over and caught his

parents before they smacked into the ground. He held them in his arms and he was the big Squirrel and theywere no more than the size of newborn pups. And they showered him with kisses and fur licking and . . .

He woke to more crying. A weak wailing, not at all Squirrel-like. Really, a mewling sound. A whimper. He threw the box back and emerged into the early morning. The dawn air still trembled with dark, and that only seemed to make the sound larger, sadder.

Though what can be sadder, Nutley thought, *than dreaming you have saved your mother and father and waking up to a different reality?*

He stood up a bit wobbly on his feet, almost as if he wasn't quite sure where he was, though actually it was the trash moving under him as it settled. *Oh for the solid earth beneath my feet or the scratch of tree bark. Even the hard pack of the Winding Road is preferable to this,* he thought. But then he scolded himself for such thinking. *I am safe here on Trash Mountain, and for now, here I will stay.*

Turning around twice, he finally located the sound. It was off in the ocean of trash reserved for the Gulls. *Well, Naw warned me about them,* he thought, turning the box back over and lying down under it again, which brought on a false dark. *Let the Gulls help their own family.* He'd had no one to help him with his.

Nutley closed his eyes. For a little while, he heard nothing but the wind puzzling through the trash and that sound very far away. The box filtered out a lot. He tried to fall asleep again. Really he did. Sleep and dreams were better than what was real. Even dreams about his parents falling. But somehow he was no longer tired.

He sighed and crawled out from under the box again.

Morning light had begun to overcome the darkness so that outside was a kind of gray. Gulls on the litter were rising up in a single great group, screaming at one another, "Mine! Mine! Mine!" and "Not yours! Not yours!" and "Give it here! Here! Here!" At the best of times, Gulls were not great thinkers, or so Father always said whenever a great cloud of them descended on the newly plowed fields of the farm. From what Nutley could hear of the Gulls' conversation, Father was absolutely right.

Then the Gulls were gone, lifting up and over Trash Mountain, flying off toward the sunrise—that small line of bright light as red as the red of the roses that climbed on Mrs. Temple's pergola—and toward fields where the early harvesters had most likely already spread out a great breakfast for them.

Nutley felt a sudden pang of jealousy. *If only I really*

was a Flying Squirrel, he thought. I'd join the Gulls, even though they have little to say. I'd fly above the Grays and bombard them with old corncobs and pieces of hard trash. I'd . . .

But he wasn't a Flying Squirrel and he would soon be nothing at all if he didn't find something to eat. Though at least if he were nothing at all, he could join Mummy and Father in Squirrel Heaven and feast forever in God's nut trees. At that moment, it didn't seem like such a bad ending at all.

The mewling cry came again, now elevated to a kind of eerie moan. Nutley jumped straight up, spinning round till he was facing in the direction the sound had come from. In the lightening air, he could see something moving slightly in the trash ocean, rolling a bit as if on waves of litter.

Glancing over his left shoulder, Nutley saw the towering Mountaintop where the dangerous large White Box perched ominously. Looking over his right shoulder, he could see the Rats' domain. No one else was up and awake.

The Gulls were all gone. It was as if the sky had been scrubbed clean of them. They'd been called by the light, called by the lure of the harvest. Things with Wings were like that—here and gone. Nutley was on his own with the cry and whoever was making it.

But then he had a further thought: *I couldn't help my parents. I was too young, too small. How can I possibly help a stranger?*

The cry was weaker now. Nutley knew all he had to do was wait a bit, stick to his own turf, find his own food, and the cry would finally go away. As Father always said, "Nature is bigger and crueler than all of us." But it hadn't been Nature that killed Father and Mummy. It had been the cruel, drunken Grays.

Was *not doing* something that leads to a death the same as *doing* it? That was the kind of question that grown-ups puzzled over. But Nutley had never had to think about any such thing before.

"I am *not* like the Grays," Nutley said. "I am a Red, and we . . ." He was not sure what Red Squirrels were. Father had always said, "We Reds are Superior." But he had died at the hands of an inferior race, so maybe that wasn't actually true. Still, Mummy always talked of gentle persuasion and that one should leave gleanings to those less fortunate creatures. Nutley hoped someone else believed in that too, because he was now the most unfortunate creature he knew.

Still, he thought, his mind wrestling with doing and not doing, I cannot just listen to that cry all day. And then his stomach growled at him, and he thought, I cannot rely on the kindness of strangers to feed me or tell me—like Naw—where to go. Such kindness might never come. His paws wrangled together. What to do? What to do? But he knew what he had to do. He would just have to shift for himself.

Cocking his head to one side, he once more thought about the Gulls' ocean of litter. If the Gulls were really and truly gone for the time being, maybe—just maybe—there would be food in that great sea of trash. He could look for food and find whoever was crying at the same time.

Double trouble, double solution. Neither Mummy nor Father had ever said that. It was his very own original thought.

In the end, though, it was really Nutley's stomach that decided him, not his kind heart. He slid down the tumble of litter onto the undulating gray and white sea to look for food.

The whimpering had stopped. In some ways, he was glad of that. And yet sorry too. After all, he *was* a true Red. Kindness was in his makeup. It was just that food was more on his mind at the moment. Food and fear.

Scurrying about in the ocean of trash, Nutley sniffed carefully and dug even more deeply than he would have done had he been burying a nut. In a very short time he'd discovered several bitter vegetables, something fishy wrapped in paper that smelled so nasty he left it, and half a container of something covered with a savory brown sauce. After stuffing himself with the vegetables dipped in the sauce—a taste he'd never tried before—he lay down on his side; curled his tail around his body; and closed his eyes, ready for more sleep.

Just then, the mewling cries started up again, and now they were very close by. For a moment, Nutley considered simply stuffing the end of his tail in his upside ear. He used to do that in the fir tree when the Grays were rioting late into the night. But these cries were not by the horrible Grays but by someone who was clearly in distress. As he had been. As his parents had been.

Sighing, Nutley stood, looked around, and then saw what he'd missed before: a Gull.

The Gull was mostly gray and white just like the trash and half sunken into a kind of pocket, so it was practically invisible. There was a knot of black string tight around its yellow beak, almost but not quite hiding a strange orange-red spot on the tip. The string had somehow become wound around its body too, keeping the gray wings with their black tips tight to its side. When he went over to get a closer look, Nutley saw that a wicked-looking metal hook dangled off the tip of the Gull's beak and that the hook swung about every time the Gull moved.

"Oh my," Nutley said.

The Gull made a deep growling sound, and the hook swung about alarmingly.

"You need help." Nutley's paws shook, with anger rather than fear. *Who could have done this to the Gull?* "I'll help as much as I can."

The growl turned into a kind of squeaky sigh.

"But you *will* have to be quiet."

Shuddering visibly, the Gull went still.

Starting with the hook end, Nutley began to unwind the string carefully, though evidently not carefully enough. Twice the hook knifed into his right paw, which hurt horribly, but he kept at it. Father would have been proud.

When he'd gotten most of the string off the Gull's beak, he hit a knot. Stepping back, he looked at the knot from several sides. Finally, he knew what was needed.

"I'm going to have to bite through this," he warned. The Gull's eyes looked wild. "Don't worry. I'm not going to bite *you*! I don't eat meat." Though he knew Gulls did. Mummy warned of it: *Flattened fauna they call it. Road kill.*

The Gull whimpered, then lay unmoving.

Using his strong front teeth, Nutley bit the knot

in two. It took but a moment. "There."

"About time," the Gull said, in a low voice, not at all sweet.

"Thanks to you too."

"Oh, manners is it?" the Gull said. "I'd like to see your manners after lying about trussed up like a Sunday roast all night and half the day long."

It was hardly half a day, but Nutley wasn't about to argue with the Gull, who was twice his size anyway. Instead, he asked: "What's a Sunday roast?"

"Never looked in a window, sonny?"

Actually, Nutley had never been allowed anywhere near Farmer Temple's house. Mummy had been adamant on that point. He shook his head.

"What *do* they teach young ones nowadays," mused the Gull, "I do wonder. In my time, it was 'Learn all you can.'"

Now *that* surprised Nutley. He'd been taught that Gulls couldn't learn anything. Father had been quite positive about it.

"Close your cakehole, sonny boy, and finish the job," the Gull said. Nutley assumed the Gull meant that he should close his mouth, which he promptly did, before going grimly back to the string.

"There's lots you Squirrels don't know about the world, scampering around all day with your noses

to the ground," the Gull said as Nutley furiously gnawed on the string.

Nutley wanted to say: *We also climb trees and look at the sky. And some of us—some of us—even fly.* But he didn't. It wouldn't have been polite. And besides, his mouth was too busy trying to free the ungrateful Gull.

The string was wound so tightly around the Gull's trembling body that once, twice, and three times more Nutley had to bite through. Only this time, he had the Gull razzing him at every bite.

"Not so close, you bugger!" said the Gull. "Nuts to you, Squirrel kin!" Without taking an extra breath, the Gull also called him a "grubber, sharper, gulpy, lurker, and lowlife."

That did it! Nutley sat back, the Gull only half unbound. "I am *not* a Lowlife, you miserable Gull."

The Gull gave a cawing laugh. "Only trying to push you on, lad. Just a Gull's way. Know you're trying your best."

"Calling names is hardly going to make me go faster," Nutley told the Gull sternly. "Father always said that the word *encourage* carries its own brave heart."

"Just the Gull's way," the Gull repeated apologetically. Its yellow eyes looked sharply at him. "We do a lot of trash-talking. But we know a lot too. However, I'll shut up if that will give you courage. And encourage you. Go for it, then." After that last outburst, the Gull stayed silent.

Nutley finished off the rest of the string in three bites. The Gull opened its wings slowly as if expecting a bit of hidden string somewhere that might catch it unawares. This close to the large bird, Nutley had to admire the Gull's gray and black wings. They were beautiful, both the individual feathers and the entire wing structure. They looked soft and strong at the same time. He suddenly wondered what it would be like to have such wings.

The Gull stood up on sturdy pinkish legs and pumped its wings. Once, twice. Nutley's fur was blown about from the wind of it. Then the Gull rose quickly into the air, banked, and headed away at a rapid rate.

"So much for thanks," Nutley called after the bird as it took off towards the harvest fields. *But that is just like a Gull*, he supposed. *No graciousness or gratitude.* He remembered Mummy saying that. Though not about Gulls, about Gray Squirrels. *But if the fur fits . . .*

Then, too tired and too angry to weep, Nutley just sat back on his haunches and watched the Gull disappear. He feared he might have gone past the point of helping himself, having used up more energy than he had taken in with food. *Perhaps*, he thought, *perhaps I will disappear as well.* In the daylight it was not as inviting a thought as it had been in the dark.

All of a sudden, the Gull was back, hovering overhead, before dropping something at Nutley's feet. It was a small hazelnut branch with five nuts still attached. Nutley was astonished. And happy. More astonished than happy, actually.

He looked up and called out, "Thanks," but he doubted the Gull heard, for it was already halfway back to the harvest fields to join its flock, those strong wings rowing the air, propelling it forward at tremendous speed.

Taking the branch in his mouth, Nutley slowly made his way back to his own space in small, tired jumps. There he got three nuts opened and ate them in a series of breathless gulps. Then, with the branch clutched tightly in his paws, just as he used to do with his acorn doll, he lay down in the box without even turning it back over, curled his tail up next to his side, and fell asleep. He slept so soundly, he didn't hear the flock of Gulls returning that evening in noisy profusion, screaming out, "Here! Here! Here!" and "Mine! Mine! Mine!" And he didn't feel any of the vibrations as they landed on the black-and-white ocean of trash.

But when he woke and ate the two remaining nuts, he called out in a sleepy voice, "Thanks!" hoping that the one Gull, his Gull—the Gull he had rescued and who had rescued him in return—had heard.

This *you* *should* *know:*

Hazelnuts are small trees,

common in moist thickets or

in the borders of woodlands.

Oddly, the budding flowers

are called catkins, though

Cats have nothing to do with

them, and they make a fruit

that is the hazelnut, also

called a filbert, or cobnut.

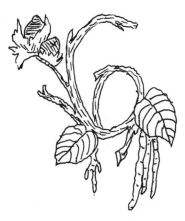

Names are one of life's mysteries that Squirrels have never pieced together. Red Squirrels are crazy about hazelnuts. How the Gull knew this is another mystery. But Gulls can fly over land and sea, and they have seen an awful lot. Who can fathom how much they truly know?

The Hazelnut Trees

When Nutley woke again, it was the next morning. The Gulls had already left for the fields. The sky was gray and lowering.

"Gray skies in the morning, Squirrels take warning," Father always said. But Nutley didn't believe that anymore. After all, here he was—alive, safe, and full.

Instead of take a warning, why not take a chance? He leaped up and spun around. But a chance on what?

Climbing on a little hillock of trash, Nutley managed to look over to the dark expanse of the Winding Road. He saw what in his hasty escape the evening before he hadn't noticed: The Spur Road ran alongside the fence. And on its north side was a moist thicket, and it was lined with hazelnut trees. That must have been where the Gull had gotten the thank-you branch.

And then Nutley did a double take. *Lined with hazelnut trees!* He could live here on Trash Mountain safe for . . . well, forever. Once or twice a day, he could cross the Road—carefully, of course—and carry back enough to eat. He stopped to consider that trip. Presumably he would go first thing in the morning and last thing at night. Dangerous but Doable. He said that aloud. "Dangerous but Doable." He bared his teeth and did a little happy dance, and the trash hillock shifted beneath his feet, but not enough to be worrisome.

Since it was still early in the morning, Nutley figured he could make a trial run without any interference. He knew he should go *around* the Rats' space. He'd been warned about that by Naw. But going around would take too long, so he decided to go right through it but be as quiet as possible. Though he trembled a bit thinking about Naw and his bride Nawmer and all the little Naws, too many to remember. What if they woke up and became angry? His tail twitched, but he knew he would have to chance the trip straight across. Just this once.

He started off, almost at a crawl. As he hoped, the Rats were late-nighters and none of them came up to interrupt his journey. He speeded up and soon was safely past the Rats' pungent space. Looking back over his shoulder, he let out a deep breath he hadn't even been aware of holding, before slipping through the Squirrel-sized openings in the wire fence.

Stopping at the side of the Spur Road, Nutley looked both ways, as Mummy always counseled, and then considered his options. Here was the Danger zone. He knew that People Carriers could come around curves with terrible speed. His Uncle Ake had died that way. And Cousin Burrower had lost a tail to one of those hurtling Carriers, which left him so cold in the winter that he'd eventually died of Freeze.

Looking left, then right, and then left again, Nutley gathered his courage. Then, in five tremendous leaps, he raced across the Spur Road. When he got to the other side, he looked up and up and up. The hazelnut trees, heavily laden with jacketed nuts, were spread like great tents above him. Heaven!

If I come over three times each day, not just twice, he thought, *I could bring back enough nuts to bury and so get through the winter.* He knew that even on Trash Mountain winter would surely come.

Quickly climbing the smallest tree, he pulled

off two nuts from the first sprig he found. The nuts cracked open easily, and the fresh kernels were fatty and full of autumn goodness. He took a moment just to savor them.

All at once he heard a frightening sound. He looked around but saw nothing to alarm him. But as if suddenly aware of the time passing, he stuffed four more nuts into his cheeks, then headed back down.

He hardly looked both ways before stepping off onto the road, and that was a mistake. Vibrations were pounding underfoot, confusing him, and luckily, he leapt back under the tree.

A pair of People Carriers whizzed by, going in two different directions, passing each other right by the foot of the tree where Nutley cowered. The wind from the passing Carriers made the fur on his back stand straight up and his ear tufts quiver. The People Carriers were going so fast that they were quickly out of sight.

Nutley was now in no hurry to set foot on the road again. But each minute away from the safety of Trash Mountain was a long one. Finally, he could delay no longer and stepped gingerly onto the road, cocking both ears and straining to feel any rumbles beneath his feet. He looked left, right, left. And for good measure, he looked around again. Then he raced back toward Trash Mountain. All the while he was on the hard gray road his heart beat so fast that he feared it would leap from his chest.

***

Nutley slipped through the fence and was so relieved to be safe again, he forgot to go around the Rats' pong-smelling hillock. Instead, he went in strong leaps across. Still, he was surprised to see Naw standing upright at the bottom of the hill, paws resting on his rather ample belly as he chewed something long and green and rotten. There was a small baby Rat sitting on his feet.

"You don't listen well, do you, Nut-Boy?" Naw said.

"I'm not actually planning to *stay* in the Rats' space," Nutley said as pleasantly as possible, though with that many nuts in his cheeks, his words were a bit indistinct. "Just going home the quickest way." *Home.* He was surprised that he already considered that wooden box in a hill of trash his home. But in fact, it was all the home he had . . . now.

As if understanding, Naw nodded. "Now, I be an easy going Rat," he said. "Can't say as much for my neighbors. The Tatters, I calls them, because they be so ragged in everything, including their opinions.

Hah!" He laughed at his own poor joke. "But I warn you, Nutter, there's those who consider North of Road their own."

"Nutley," Nutley said. "My name is Nutley."

"Nutley, Nutter, sounds the same when you have too many nuts in your cheeks," Naw told him. Then he repeated his warning. "Beware—there's those who consider North of Road their own." At his feet, the baby Rat squealed and clapped its paws.

Nutley would have gulped at the warning, but he really *was* carrying too many nuts in his cheeks, as Naw had so rightly noted. And that made gulping Dangerous. It was one of the first rules a young Squirrel learns. "Who?" he asked faintly.

"Who what?" asked Naw, smiling down at the young Rat. He dropped a strand of the green stuff on purpose. The little Rat grabbed it up and began to nibble.

"Who considers North of Road their own?" *Really,* Nutley thought, *this was a most annoying conversation. Father would have had something severe to say about it.*

"Didn't I just say the Tatters?" Naw winked. First, at the baby Rat and then at Nutley. One long wink. It was an awful wink, his eyelid laboring to get back up again as if it was too old for such a climb. "Got nuts in your ears?"

The little Rat at his feet started giggling at the joke. It sounded like a wheeze crossed with a gasp, as if the poor thing was going to die of laughter. Naw picked it up and pounded it on the back, then rocked the baby in his arms till it was still. "Hush, Nawshus," he crooned in a squeaky tenor voice till the baby did, indeed, hush and fall asleep, snoring lightly, the strand of green stuff hanging from its open mouth.

Nutley marveled at how tender the old Rat seemed to be, which was so at odds with his long nose, his big teeth, and the green stuff sticking out of his jaws. He reminded Nutley, somehow, of Father, though they were nothing alike.

"Get on now," said Naw. "There's plenty enough to eat on the Mountain. No need to cross over. No need to go off your turf. No need indeed." Then he turned, and—with the baby under his right arm—he burrowed into the trash and was gone.

But there is *need,* Nutley thought. *Need for a Squirrel at any rate.* Everyone knew Red Squirrels were not naturally eaters of trash, not like Rats or Gulls. Besides, the lure of the nut trees was too strong. Now that he knew they were just across the road, he could even smell them over the Rats' pongy hillock. Nothing in the fuddling place could compete with the scent of those trees. Nutley knew he would go back again that very night.

**

Hurrying on, Nutley found the way to his box, where he ate one of the four nuts, and buried the rest. He buried them deep enough and secretly enough so that only he would be able to find them. *Learned that from the Grays*, he thought. He snarled and acted Dangerous for a minute. Then he curled up for his morning nap.

He slept longer than he'd meant to, for when he woke, the sun had crossed over the nut trees. The Gulls were already starting to arrive back from the harvest fields, calling to one another in their coarse, indistinguishable voices.

"Mine. Mine. Mine." Their wing flaps got closer. "Mine. Mine. Mine."

He wondered if all Gulls knew more than they showed or just the one Gull he'd saved. His Gull had been talkative though—if truth be told, as Mummy said it always should—the Gull had also been rather rude. But still, Nutley *had* been thanked for his heroism. And given presents of nuts. That counted for a lot.

A shadow fell on him, dark and ominous. He looked up frightened. Even though it was day, not night when Owls came out, a shadow from above was never a good thing. It could be a Kite, a Harrier, a Hawk, or a Buzzard. As Mummy had taught him:

Wings from above
Never bring love.

He could feel the wind from those wings and was about to dive under the box when he heard a familiar voice.

"Yours," said the Gull, dropping another twig with three small nuts down to him.

This time, Nutley was far too astonished to call out his thanks. He simply grabbed the nuts and—as the Gull flew off—bit through the jacket of one, and contentedly munched on the sweet inner meat.

Nothing better, he thought, before burying the remaining two nuts, quite close to the others.

"Well, that's that!" he said out loud when he was done with the burying, as if there was someone other than himself close enough to hear. "My larder for winter is certainly improving." While that was undeniably true, he knew that five nuts would not be nearly enough to carry him through an entire season of cold. And he couldn't count on the Gull feeling sorry or thankful or whatever it was Gulls feel for much longer. Not even once more.

"No," he told any unknown listeners, "I will wait until the sun is almost down and then head back to the trees."

Though this time, he promised himself, *I will avoid going through the Rats' space.* He knew that they were sure to be up and about then, both Naw's family and the Tatters. And that was many more Rats than he was comfortable to meet at one time, even if the majority of them were babies.

This you should know:
Red Squirrels are pretty
straightforward about burying
nuts. But Grays make fake burials
to fool anyone who might be
watching. Some scientists call this
a form of intelligence. Others say
that means Grays are devious and
underhanded. Some believe that
nut-burying is not food storage
at all since Squirrels have warm,

dry shelters where they could easily stash their winter food. For these scientists, Squirrels are the original nut farmers, carefully planting nuts so that new nut trees can grow. That may be a leap, but really—how much do we really know about Squirrels?

Name-Calling

Before his evening trip, Nutley unearthed one of the hazelnuts he'd buried and ate it slowly, eyes closed, savoring each bite. As he chewed, he thought about all the tastes the nut had—a musty sweetness on the outside and a tang as he got closer to the center. Then the chewy nugget that burst with hidden sunshine. Oh, how he loved hazelnuts.

He considered unburying a second onebut then remembered that soon enough, once he was back at the trees, he'd have plenty to choose from. That was the problem with knowing where your nuts were buried. They sat in their little burrows singing the *Come-and-Get-Me* song that was so hard to resist. Mummy called it "the lure of the nut." And Father said, "You mean the *allure*." It was something that made them both laugh. Nutley smiled at the memory.

"You there, Nut-Muncher," came a familiar voice, knifing through his reverie. "Stop being a shirkster, and ope the orbs."

"Gull!" Nutley said, opening his eyes. "Sir, I've been wanting to thank you."

"Thanks open no banks," said the Gull. "And besides, I'm no Sir but a Lady."

"You are? I'm sorry. I'm . . ." He was going to say *embarrassed* but never got a chance to because the Gull interrupted him.

"You can tell because we female Gulls are lighter-colored and smaller. And smarter too. But I can't expect a Squirrel to know that. *Fuzzy-Tails of Little Brain*, my Mum called you. Knew this right from the egg, I did, along with my two brothers. Though Mum did say Reds were nicer than the thieving Grays, them egg suckers."

"Well, my parents called you Gulls 'Flying Rats.'"

"Flying Rats. I wonder who should be more insulted, Naw and his gang or me and my kin?" She chuckled, a kind of *kyee-kyee-kyee* sound. "Now we've got the name-calling out of the way, I'll tell you why I've come back." Her yellow eyes sparkled. There was an odd orange ring around them. "If you have a wish, Nut-Boy, I'll grant it if I can. You saved my life. Thanks a bunch. Name's Larie."

Nutley trembled, furious with himself that the Gull had been more gracious than he. He couldn't call back all that he'd said to her, but he could tell her his name. "Not Nut-Boy—Nutley," he said.

"Ho! Then Nutley, here's to you. You saved me when others—who shall remain nameless though I know their names, every one—left me lying there trussed like a Christmas roast." Larie's wings stretched out, and she pecked at one, shaking out a loose feather. Then she snapped her wings shut tight against her sides, which sounded a little like *whoosh, whap.* "Gulls don't forget their mates." She gave a loud cry and looked over her right shoulder, calling out, "At least some of us don't!" She stretched her wings again.

Thinking about a wish, Nutley ventured, "Have you ever heard of Flying Squirrels?"

"Heard of 'em? I've *seen* them."

"Around here?"

Larie let out a raucous laugh. *Kyee-kyee-kyee.* "This is Britain," she said. "Most Flying Squirrels live far across the sea. In the Americas, both North and South."

Nutley's jaw dropped. "You've been across the sea?"

She shook out her wings again. "These things.

Gray with feathers? Called wings. Whadda they mean? Flight." *Kyee-kyee-kyee.* She laughed again and snapped her wings shut. *Whoosh, whap.* "We've been called *Sea* Gulls. Sea, ocean, got it, Nutley? I mean, really—I've heard Squirrels weren't too sharp, but that takes the cake." She shook herself out again. "Tell me, really—whadda you think?"

She sure talks a lot about cakes, Nutley thought, but didn't say that out loud. And then he smiled. He knew what he thought. Gulls were a *lot* smarter than Father said. *Or at least Larie was.* He didn't say that either. "Tell me about Flying Squirrels then. About *their* wings."

"Not real wings, Nutley. Not real fliers. They should be called *Gliding* Squirrels." Another golden twinkle of her eye.

"Oh," said Nutley. He wouldn't mind gliding either. It sounded interesting. Possibly Dangerous.

Larie stretched her wings once more. She picked up her left leg, then set it down. She picked up her right. It almost looked as if she were dancing. "Gotta go! Gotta go! Maybe I'll take you flying someday, Nut-Boy."

"Nutley," said Nutley.

Larie laughed. *Ark, ark, ark.*

"Soon?" Nutley asked.

"Maybe sooner than that," Larie said, somewhat mysteriously. Then, with a flapping of her great gray wings, the black tips waving at him like flags, she was gone once again.

"And I should be gone too," Nutley told himself, glancing at the darkening sky. He'd dillied and dallied too long talking to the Gull. If he was going to get back to the hazelnuts before night closed in, he had to leave. Now.

***

Nutley crept around the outskirts of Trash Mountain, far away from any spaces claimed by Rats, Gulls, or other unnamed creatures and close to the wire fence. The light was already smudgy, that interim time before real dark.

"Dark is Danger," he said, quoting Father. At least in that, Father was absolutely right.

Nutley slipped through the same hole in the wire fence he'd used before. Once on the other side, he sniffed the air carefully. This air was closer than the air at Temple's farm, heavier somehow, compounded of the trash smell (though he had gotten used to that) and the moist thicket across the road that had its own deep, earthy, mulchy, wet odor. And the river as well. The ground beneath the fir tree had sometimes smelled that way, but only after days of soaking rain.

He raced to the edge of the Spur Road and stopped. Ear to the Road, he heard nothing to prevent him from crossing. No unusual sounds, no vibrations. He took a deep breath and—with five big leaps and a skittering run at the end—he was over.

With the sunset behind them, the hazelnut trees cast strange shadows, like dark Trolls with huge fingers. Mummy loved to tell stories about Trolls. As a pup she had often listened when Farmer Temple's wife read stories to her grandchildren on the porch. That was long before the Grays had come, of course. And back when the Reds were not lumped in with the Grays as Nuisances to be kept off the porch by various means. But Mummy was always careful to say to Nutley at the end of such stories, "Isn't it lucky trolls don't really exist."

Lucky indeed, Nutley thought. He had enough trouble worrying about the Grays. And Things with Wings. And Night Creatures. "Nocturnal Enemies," Father called them. And the dreaded People Carriers.

He made his way to the familiar smallest

tree and scrambled up.

For a moment he sat in the tree without thinking, just loving the feel of the branch below his feet, the bumpiness of bark. Then he sniffed the crisp air. The wind was behind him and blowing toward Trash Mountain, which meant that he was getting the tang off the open fields behind instead of any lingering smell from the tip.

"Ah," he whispered, the sound round and satisfying as a nut in his mouth.

Finally, he reached over and broke off two nuts. Cracking them open, he ate the nutmeat quickly, savoring them, but not lingering over the tastes as he had in the safety of his box. In the coming dark, he didn't trust the North of the Road trees. And once the sun went down behind the hills, it would be full night.

Night *was* Dangerous. Scary. Full of beaks and talons. Full of spilled blood. Munchings of meat. Crunchings of bone. One needn't be a Squirrel to know this. If he concentrated on the nuts, maybe—just maybe—he could let go of his fear.

This you should know:
Not all Night Creatures are
Dangerous to Squirrels. Bats,
Nightjars, Moths, Fireflies,
Crickets, Millipedes, Badgers,
Rats, Hedgehogs, Mice, even Deer
live side by side with Squirrels
without any animosity. But the
night has many sharp teeth and
talons. No Squirrel ever feels
safe when dark closes in. None.

Night Trees

The wind settled. The evening air was still. Nutley had just started breaking off a branch with five nuts to take back with him, when he heard a soft sound below the tree. A *scritch*. Then a *scratch*. Then a scrabbling sound. He remembered with a shiver what Naw had warned. *There's those who consider North of Road their own.*

Nutley wondered if Naw had meant Rats. Or Gulls. Or Foxes. Or even People. People sometimes came out of their houses or stopped their Carriers. Some of them even walked along the Winding Road, and occasionally they walked with huge animals on strings. "Hounds," Father called them. "Dogs" is what Mummy said. According to both of them, though, Hounds/Dogs liked to chase Squirrels. Nutley tried to make himself invisible in the uppermost leaves of the hazelnut tree and wondered if Hounds/Dogs also liked to climb trees. He knew Cats could.

The sounds came again. *Scritch. Scratch. Scrabble.* Something was scrambling around at the base of the tree, and the noise traveled up the bark in waves.

Startled, Nutley dropped the little branch he was holding, and it hit the tree trunk and then several large limbs, knocking off two of the nuts as it fell. Down and down and . . . Nutley leaned over, almost mesmerized, and watched it fall.

Someone snatched the branch up in mid-flight. Nutley couldn't make out who or what had grabbed it. But more important, he hoped who or what hadn't seen him.

He heard a loud crack as if someone had chewed through one of the nuts. Then there was a flurry of howls and chittering from below.

It can't be! he thought. *How could they be here? How could they know?*

"Whoever you are up there, come on down ye weenie and fight like a Gray. These trees are ours!"

Ours? Nutley felt cold all over. His ear tufts drooped. *There was more than one of them on the ground below?* Nutley couldn't think what to do. How far along the Winding Road had the Grays spread? All the way to the Spur Road? Were these the same crew who'd killed Mummy and Father, or were they uncles and cousins of that lot? And really—did it matter? Grays were Grays. Mean and unsharing, uncaring and ready to fight. He didn't dare stay any longer.

Pulling himself back against the trunk till he all but blended in and thanking the Squirrel Gods that it was dusk and that red was a dark color, Nutley tried to make a plan. But his head was as fuddled as the trash where he lived. He had plenty of questions, but not one good answer.

Could he leap from tree to tree faster? Being lighter than the Grays might actually be an advantage in the treetops. But what if they all started climbing? What if there were enough of them to get up into all the trees, trapping him between?

And what would happen when he ran out of trees?

He began to shiver with fear, cold rivers running through his skin. His tail thrashed about. His paws wrangled. *Why, oh why did I ever leave Trash Mountain?* He worked hard at not whimpering. Whimpering would give him away.

Oh, Mummy, oh, Father, he thought. Suddenly he knew that he wanted desperately to live, that he was too young to die. And with those thoughts uppermost in his mind, he left the momentary safety of the tree trunk; raced to the farthest end of the farthest, bendiest branch of the tree, and leapt to the next tree and then the next.

A People Carrier, lights blazing, turned onto the Spur Road below him, and Nutley heard the Grays scattering. One—he hoped it was more than one actually—screamed as the big round things ran over it. But as soon as the Carrier was gone, the Grays were back again, surrounding the very tree that Nutley was now perched in, chittering their threats once more.

And then Nutley thought, *Maybe they will let me come down if I promise to stay in the trash. Surely they would find it amusing that I would volunteer to stay there and . . .*

"Come down! Come down and meet your fate!" someone called. Nutley thought it sounded like Groundling. *If it is,* he realized, *then these are the same Grays who killed Mummy and Father and they will never let me go. Never.*

Another voice cried, "We know you're there, Nutley!" Soon they had all taken up the call. "Nutley! Nutley! Nutley!"

How do they know which tree I'm in? he wondered. *How do they know it's me?*

Then he realized that he was shaking so hard with

fear that the top of the tree where he perched was swaying, even though there wasn't any wind. As for how they knew it was he—why they could smell Reds just as he could smell Grays. *What other Red Squirrels were around? They probably killed any others long ago.* His tail twitched. *Maybe Mummy and Father and I were the very last.* It wasn't a comforting thought.

"Go away!" he started to call out, before realizing this would just encourage them more. And that's when he heard the Grays start scrambling up the very tree he was hiding in.

Nutley looked over at the next hazelnut tree. It was, perhaps, a bit too far for him to jump. But still he had to try. He couldn't go back. There were Grays in the first three trees already. They were sure to grab him, and now there were even more coming up from right below.

He had *no* choice. None.

Closing his eyes, he tried to visualize himself as a Flying Squirrel—no, a *Gliding* Squirrel, whatever that was. He edged out onto the thinnest, furthermost branch. Not even a branch. A twig. He held his arms wide as if they were wings and prepared to leap into the air.

There was a quiet flap above him. *How did the Grays get up above me?* he wondered. *The branches there are even too thin for me.*

But he had no time to wonder further. He just leapt out into the air towards the faraway tree, with hope in his teeth as if it were a nut not yet cracked.

A heavier and faster Gray leaped after him with such speed he whizzed right past Nutley in the air, then turned and reached out one paw as if to grab Nutley. As he did so, the Gray was suddenly lifted up. *Lifted!* Nutley glimpsed huge dark wings and great talons above the Gray. He felt the wind from silent wings. Opening his mouth, he tried to scream but no sound came out.

Surprised at how the scrawny Red Squirrel it had aimed for had become a different, heavier, meatier Gray, the Owl almost dropped its dinner. But giving silent thanks to the Owl gods, it grasped its prey even tighter in its talons, pumped its mighty wings, and flew off silently.

Nutley was no longer flying through the air but rather gliding—at least he thought he was gliding—which quickly turned into falling. He had a sudden vision of Father, sprawled out beneath the tree and wondered if the landing would hurt or if it would simply kill him immediately. He started to close his eyes. He had no time for prayer.

"Grab the stick, Nutley," called out a familiar

hoarse voice. "Time to go for that ride."

"Larie!" Even as he fell, Nutley peered up into the dark.

Spurred on by the voices above them, the Grays burst through the lower leaves of the tree and stared as Nutley reached one paw up for the stick he hoped was right above him.

It was.

He managed to grab it with his paw and hold on. Larie's great gray wings beat slowly as she swung him away from the tree.

The Grays began to scream slurs and bad names. "You unnatural pairing! You big white-gray Rat with wings! You flipping Flying Squirrel!"

Nutley twisted about, which was a difficult maneuver, and screamed back, "They glide, you Dumbnuts. Glide!" and he almost lost hold of the stick.

"Shut your cakehole and hold tight, Nutley," encouraged Larie. "You don't want to fall now."

Cake again, Nutley thought. *She sure likes to talk about cake*. But at the same time, he felt courage swell in his chest and he closed his left paw even more tightly around the stick. They flew away from the tree toward Trash Mountain.

This only incensed the Grays even more, and with one of them high in the tree calling instructions to the

others, they tracked Larie and Nutley as they flew over the fence and onto the gray and white litter. There was a full moon overhead, and the Gull and Squirrel were easy to see.

Larie lowered Nutley down right by his box. "You're no lightweight, kid. My legs are going to be sore for days."

"Thank you. Thank you," Nutley said. "I hope I didn't put you to any trouble."

"Trouble is what *you* have, I'm afraid." Lariegestured with her head toward the Winding Road.

In the moonlight, Nutley could see the Grays dashing across the road and heading up the dirt lane, like a great gray river of doom. Soon they would be at the fence.

"Surely, they won't come in . . ." Nutley said.

"You did."

"I had no choice."

"Maybe they have none, either," she said. "Anger sometimes puts a body in that place."

"What should I do?" Nutley asked. The gray river flowed through the fence holes and onto the patch of trash belonging to the Rats.

Before Larie could venture an answer, they both heard a huge caterwauling as Naw and

Nawmer and five Tatters boiled up out of their holes to defend their place.

"Will the Rats hold them?"

"We can only hope."

But *hope*, Nutley knew, was the one thing he had very little of.

This you should know:
Rats—especially brown Rats—
love a good trash heap. Tips,
junk piles, scrap heaps, garbage
dumps, landfills, middens, you
name it, the brown Rat will be
there. How can you know they
are there? Look for narrow, well-
used paths. Find dark, greasy
trails. Unlike Squirrels, Rats do
not bury their food. Anything

uneaten is left behind. This is

because the Rat will devour

almost anything, so they never

have to worry about going

hungry. Also, this you should

know as well: Rats are very

tolerant—of other Rats. Not so

much of outsiders.

Battle of the Rats

Riveted, Nutley and Larie watched as the Rats formed a battle line. Shoulder to shoulder, they stood on their hind legs, which made them tower over the invaders. They bared their teeth at the Squirrels. Big teeth. Very big teeth. And yellow.

Seeing that line's precision, the Grays stopped, suddenly stymied in their forward motion. Their own line was ragged, disordered, tails a-quiver. Uneasily, they glanced at one another. They'd been

expecting a straightforward romp over a defenseless Red Squirrel. Instead they got . . .

"Rats!" said one of the Grays. And the others mumbled back the same. Several clearly considered running away and glanced over their shoulders. But a low chitter from the others held them in place.

Nutley turning toward Larie. "The Rats look *really* Dangerous." He meant it in an admiring way. He bared his teeth too.

"They are," Larie told him. "And they don't share well."

"You sound like my Mummy." Nutley meant *that* in an admiring way too.

"Well, I'm *not* your Mumsy," said Larie. "Not now, not ever." She shook out her wings. "See—gray wings, yellow beak, pink legs. Whadda you think it all means, Nut-Boy?"

Nutley turned back and faced the battle again. He didn't want Larie to see how much he was blushing with embarrassment. *Red on red*, as Mummy used to say. She'd been right about Gulls. They had no manners at all.

Over on the Rats' place, the Grays had begun to shake themselves into a kind of battle order. After all, they outnumbered the Rats twelve to seven. In the Grays counting, that meant the battle was already won.

They always figured numbers gave a victory. Possibly all the other times it had.

Making a loose circle around the Rats, the Grays took turns calling out nasty chatter. Nutley knew it was a way of building up their own courage while at the same time trying to soften up the enemy. Usually—as he knew only too well—it was a strategy that worked.

"Garbage eaters!" yelled one Gray, who had a streak of white down his tail.

"Rat-a-tat-tat, your Mama's FAT!" called another. His ears stood up almost as tall as Nutley's.

"Skinny tail." cried a third.

"Skinned tail!" screamed a fourth. And indeed, to a Squirrel, a Rat's tail must have looked like it had been skinned with a knife.

And so it went around the circle.

"Pot-bellied bully!"

"Dirty ratskin."

"Tip-tipper, hit you with a slipper!"

Nutley knew that last voice. It was Groundling.

At each name, at each rhyming insult, the Rats snarled back.

A standoff, Father would have called it.

Larie poked Nutley's shoulder with her beak. "Now's the time for us to escape," she told him, "while they are concentrated on the Rats. We need to get to the top of the Mountain. To the White Box. You can hide in there. It has a Dead Man's Latch."

Nutley shuddered. He didn't like the sound of that. He didn't like the sound of *anything* with the word *Dead* in it.

"But Naw said . . ." He bit his lip hard. "Naw said *Thosethatgoesindon'tcomeoutagain.*"

Larie cocked her head to one side. "And you believe him? He's only a Rat."

Nutley's paws wrangled together. His ear tufts quivered. "Yes, but . . . but he's been nice to me, and . . ."

"And he's never been in the White Box, so what does *he* know?"

It was what Father would have called an unanswerable argument.

"Will you fly me up there?" Nutley asked, hating that there was a pleading note in his voice.

Larie shook her head. "Once a night is more than enough for a Gull to be carrying heavy objects. But you'll have a good head start while the Grays are fighting the Rats. Don't worry, the bloodshed should start soon. It'll keep them all busy. I'll meet you up there." And with a little leap and the pumping of her gray wings, she was away, shimmering in the light of the moon.

To the sound of the insults between the Rats and

the Grays—for now the Rats were hurling names back at the Squirrels—Nutley quickly unburied the nuts he'd stored and placed them in his cheeks. He might not be able to find any other food for a while. There certainly wouldn't be any in the White Box. The word *Dead* resounded in his ear. *Better to be safe than* . . . But there was nothing safe about this night at all.

Cheeks bulging, he started to turn toward the Mountain, when the sound of the name-calling behind him on the Rats' territory changed. There was a huge audible gasp. It was like a tremor in the air.

Nutley looked over his shoulder and in horror saw that the littlest Naw-baby—Nawshus—had come up out of a burrow to investigate what all the fuss was about. Only it had popped out closer to the circle of Grays than to the pack of Rats.

The Gray with the white stripe on his tail moved quickly, taking a half leap forward. His tail waved like a banner in a small wind. With a swift paw, he scooped up little Nawshus and held the baby Rat high overhead.

"Yummers!" the Gray cried and at the same time made a chewing noise, his teeth clacketing loudly against one another, as if breaking open a particularly difficult nut.

It was a horrible sound. Nutley felt a cold shiver go

down his back. Little Nawshus began to cry.

With a huge, angry yell, the Rats broke formation and Nawmer threw herself at the Gray who was holding her baby. He went over backward, and she followed, burying her large yellow teeth in his neck. Blood began to spurt.

But Nawmer was too late with her attack because even as he fell, the Gray had flung Nawshus to one side, and the Gray next to him had caught the terrified little Rat, hugging Nawshus to his chest.

One of the Tatters—a giant brown with torn ears and a crook in his tail—grabbed that Gray around the middle, biting down on his catching arm. However, just a moment before that attack, little Nawshus had been flung clear across the circle, to a female Gray whose back was to Nutley.

Nutley recognized the game. It was a favorite of the Grays—Nut Keep Away. They were good at it. Well practiced. They could continue for hours.

Now Nutley could hear the little Rat screaming in terror, "Dada! Mummy!"

Heart pounding, Nutley ran in the biggest jumps he could muster across his own territory, leaped forward, and hit the Gray right in the small of her back. No one had been expecting that. They'd forgotten all about him. Or if they thought of him at all, they assumed

he'd run away long ago. But not for a minute did Nutley think of his own Danger. He only wanted to save the little Rat.

As Nutley hit the Gray, most of the nuts in his cheeks sprayed out like shots from Farmer Temple's gun, hitting Squirrels on either side and momentarily distracting them with the tantalizing odor of hazelnuts.

Nawshus popped out of the Gray's paw, tumbling over and over till he landed at Nawmer's feet. She scooped him up in one paw and without taking time to see what else was happening, dove into a burrow in the trash and was gone.

And then the real war began. Six against twelve. Well, eleven. The Squirrel with the white on his tail was no longer moving. Nutley knew the battle wasn't going to be pretty. He struggled up off the back of the female Gray and without picking up the nuts that had sprayed over the ground, raced away. He'd done all that he could, and now he knew he had to escape.

The Rats were on their own.

This you should know:

Gulls (Latin name Laridae) come in many types: Common, Glaucous, Lesser Black-Backed, and others. The different types are quite distinctive—if you know what to look for. Larie is a Herring Gull, and in her fourth year. Loud and noisy, Herring Gulls are found throughout the year in Britain, in seaside towns, in rubbish tips, on playing fields, and on farms. Would Herring Gulls fight? They often battle other

birds for territory, gripping with their beaks, pushing and pulling with their legs, flailing with their hardy wings. Could a Herring Gull carry a Squirrel aloft? Well, a Herring Gull carries Mollusks and Crabs up to drop them on stones in order to break them open. How much heavier could a small Red Squirrel be?

Herring Gull

Larus argentatus

The Gulls' Anger

Carefully skirting the Gulls' trash ocean, Nutley raced along, keeping the towering Mountain in his sight, though it was far enough away to be just a large misty presence ahead of him. He knew it would be faster going straight across, but he didn't dare. Naw had warned him, and now Nutley believed Naw.

The Gulls were already nestling down for the night. He could see them out of the corner of his eye, fluttering and shrilly trumpeting *kyee-kyee yowk-yowk-yow.*

Even though they would soon be asleep, he didn't veer across their space. After all, the only Gull who was actually his friend was Larie, and she was already winging toward the Great White Box. Indeed, she was probably there. So she couldn't speak to her family on his behalf. And without her vouching for him, it was too Dangerous.

As he circled the Gulls' space, Nutley's breath came in sharp, painful gasps. Now he could hear some of the Grays behind him, panting furiously, the pattering of their feet more than matching the speed of his own. And he thought he could distinguish as well some of them off to the side. He had no idea how many Grays there were, whether there were two or lots. Whether they had beaten the Rats utterly or had just escaped from the Rats' strong teeth. It didn't matter. He couldn't take the time to check.

Fear made Nutley speed up. But anger was helping the Grays. And now it was clear that some of them were taking the Dangerous shortcut across the Gulls' territory. He could see them out of the corner of one eye. In another leap or three, they would cut him off.

Terror lent him strength, but it didn't lend him wings. *And alas*, thought Nutley, *only wings can save me now.*

But the nestling Gulls were already half asleep. Even had they been awake, Nutley wondered what—if anything—they could or would do. This wasn't their fight, after all.

He would have called for help but remembered

the Gulls hadn't even helped Larie, their sister, their friend. And he had little time to consider any other course of action as the Grays closed in on him.

Suddenly, from the midst of the Gulls' space, there was a huge *whoshing* sound, and a great gray cloud rose up. The Gulls might not want to help Nutley and they didn't help one of their own when she was trussed up and possibly dying, but it seems they were more than ready to defend their territory. Nutley was astonished and thankful, in equal measure.

For a moment they hovered, and it was eerily silent except for Gulls. And only Nutley—now rounding the corner and heading straight for the Mountain and in a crash course toward the over-landing Grays—only Nutley noticed the cloud of birds.

And then the Gulls dived down on the invading Grays, screaming, "Mine! Mine! Mine!" Their yellow bills glowed in the moonlight like light sabers. Nutley knew about light sabers. It was one of the stories Mummy had heard on the porch when Farmer Temple's wife read to her grandchildren. Nutley liked that story better than the ones about Trolls.

The Gulls speared the Gray Squirrels with their sharp beaks. And the larger Gulls managed to grab up five of the smaller, lighter Squirrels by their tails, flying them over the fence and dropping them onto the Winding Road as if they were merely clamshells they were trying to open.

What the Rats had begun, it seemed as if the Gulls would finish.

"Mine! Mine! Mine!" the gray cloud squawked as it flew back down to its bed in the trash. Then with a last fluttering of wings, they settled in for the night.

Only four of the Grays had been smart enough to come the long way around, following Nutley. Maybe three or four of them. Nutley couldn't tell. He kept running as fast as he could until finally he had to stop to catch his breath. His legs trembled, and there was a searing pain along his right side. Taking in great gulps of air, he was surprised to find he still had two nuts left in his cheeks. But he didn't have time to eat them, and besides now—suddenly—he had a plan. Turning, he spit the two nuts out behind him, then began running again.

The first of the Grays on his trail found his spit-out stash and shouted, "Nuts!" The lure of free food overcame him, and he squatted right down to eat. But the three remaining Grays paid no attention and kept running after their prey.

Nuts! Nutley thought. He'd hoped the nuts would have slowed them down. That they would stop and fight over the little stash. But there were three still

after him, Grays bigger and stronger and faster. Now he was sure he wouldn't make it; he simply could not take another leap. *At least*, he thought, *at least I will be with Mummy and Father.* He stopped, turned, closed his eyes, and waited for the teeth in his throat.

And then something grabbed him by the tail.

How could that be? He wondered if some Gray had sneaked behind him. And then he began a chittering scream. He screamed and screamed until he realized he was being lifted. He twisted around and looked up at the glowing gray wings beating above him.

"Larie," he cried, "I'm too heavy. You said so. Drop me. Save yourself."

"Stop wingeing, Nut-Boy," came the reply.

He stopped wingeing, whatever that was, but he closed his eyes, crossed his front paws, and didn't dare open his eyes again until Larie said, "Landing now."

Nutley didn't worry about the landing. The bottom of his tail, where it attached to his rear, hurt too badly to worry about anything.

"Ow," he said, once all four of his feet were again on the ground. "Ow." If he hoped for sympathy from the Gull, he was mistaken.

Larie was too busy looking around to offer any. "All clear," she said at last. "Now hurry."

Nutley opened his eyes in surprise.

This you should know:
Dumping old washers and dryers
in landfills is environmentally
unsafe. Thousands of such
machines sit like death traps
in these places, and it takes
them hundreds of years before
they begin to degrade. Yet
sometimes magic happens
there. Or power. Think of
all that energy lying about
untapped in those appliance
graveyards, waiting to spark

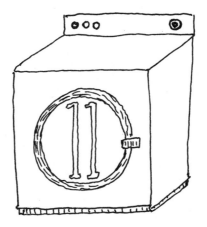

to life. Scattered about Trash
Mountain are half-used batteries,
undischarged capacitors, tangled
wires, standing pools of water.
Lightning may not strike the
same place twice, but for Nutley,
once may be enough.

The Great White Box

The two of them were now up at the very top of Trash Mountain. From that height, Nutley sensed the moon almost touching his shoulder. He looked up. It was an enormous presence, big and round and orange. He had only seen it once before. *Harvest Moon*, Mummy called it.

Though the only thing it seemed to be harvesting at the moment were clouds. Dark gray clouds, racing toward it. He thought there might be a storm coming, which could complicate things even more.

But as he looked around, he realized that he and Larie were alone at the top. Very alone.

"We're safe!" he cried. "Safe." He ignored his stinging bottom, his still-pounding heart, and he even ignored the first rumble of faraway thunder.

"Safe for the moment," Larie told him.

In front of them stood the Great White Box. Or rather, in front of them teetered the Great White Box. Its door, with the round window, swung open invitingly. There was something eerie about it.

Nutley heard a noise and looked about. Suddenly, he noticed a shadowy movement at the bottom of the tottery mountain of trash. Three gray shapes with long, waving tails. He guessed—no, he *knew*–that they were the Grays. Trying to climb up the sides of the Mountain, they kept slipping back. All the while they cursed loudly, calling him names, like "Weenie" and "Rat Lover" as well as words he'd never even heard before so had no idea what they meant, like "Fink" and "Flabbergaster." Then they rested for a moment before trying to climb up again. It reminded him of the stories Father liked to tell about the Great Salmon, some mythical Fish that spent much of its life trying to leap *up* waterfalls. Which sounded unlikely to Nutley. The Grays seemed to be having as much luck getting to the top of Trash Mountain as the Great Salmon had getting to the top of the Falls.

The moment he thought of the *Falls*, the gray clouds opened up and a waterfall of rain began to wash around them. It bucketed down. There were clashes and flashes of lightning on both sides that lit up the landscape.

Hope fountained into Nutley's heart. He and Larie could remain on the Mountain and maybe shelter just inside the Great White Box without needing to close the door at all while the Grays got so wet and tired they would finally have to give up. Once the rain stopped, Larie could fly off and bring him back nuts and they would be fine, and . . .

"Get in," said Larie, snapping her beak for emphasis and pointing a wing at the Great White Box.

That was when Nutley remembered what Larie had told him about what waited inside. *A Dead Man's Latch.*

And then he remembered too what Naw had said about the White Box. "*Thosethatgoesindon'tcomeoutagain.*"

"We don't actually have to do anything," he told her. "Look—the Grays can't get up here. Not with the Mountain going all slippery with this storm, and . . ."

"*That* side," she whispered. "They can't get up *that* side. But sooner or later, they'll find out that the back side is easier. A gentler slope."

"How do you know . . ." Nutley began. Then nodded. "Right—wings. You've flown over and seen it."

In the lightning flashes, Larie's yellow eyes

sparked. "Even a Squirrel can figure that out ... eventually." Then she cocked her head to one side, clearly listening.

Nutley didn't even bother arguing, because now he could make out the sounds Larie heard—someone was already scrambling up the back side of the Mountain. So the Grays *had* figured it out. Sooner rather than later.

Several voices were now shouting up at them. "We'll get you yet, you thieving weenie." He could hear them panting and hollering in turns, coming closer and closer.

"Don't be a Dumbnut," Larie said. "Get into the Great White Box."

"But ... Naw ... *Thosethatgoesindon'tcomeoutagain*," Nutley's voice broke twice on the long word, but he was too frightened to care.

"What's there to come out for?" asked Larie.

He knew she was right. He hated that she was right. He hopped into the Great White Box. Larie hopped in with him.

"But you can fly away ... " Nutley said. "You can go back down to your mates. You can escape. Be free. Be safe."

"So I can," she answered. "But they weren't no mates of mine when I needed them most. Only you were."

150

Nutley didn't say anything more. Actually, he was relieved. If he had to be somewhere he couldn't come out of again, it was best to be there with a friend.

Larie settled down inside the Box, adding, "Besides, I love adventure. Trust me, Nut-Nerd, I've seen a lot. This one promises to be the most interesting adventure of them all."

He wasn't sure he liked that—about an adventure that promised to be interesting. *Interesting* meant Danger. He was tired of Danger. He just wanted quiet. Peace. Friendship.

And nuts.

So he reached out to grab the back of the door to pull it shut, but it was suddenly flung wide open and a body hurtled in.

"Gotcha!" came a familiar voice.

Nutley knew at once it was Groundling. *It is going to be,* he thought, *an ignoble end after all.* But the one he was most worried about was Larie. He hadn't been able to save Mummy or Father, but now he knew where his duty lay.

He had to save Larie!

As Groundling rushed in, even before he could turn around and savage either one of them, Nutley grabbed him by the tail. Using every ounce of strength he had, Nutley swung the Gray against the Box wall.

There was a loud *crack!*

Groundling crumpled and lay still.

At the same time, something rustled by his side.

He heard a t*hunk* and then a *click*. "What?" he began.

"Shutting the door, Nut-Boy," Larie said. "Quick now. The latch."

"But we need to throw him—" he gestured to the crumpled Groundling—"out."

"We don't want more of those Gray Ghouls coming in here. What we *need* is not to make things any more interesting than they already are." Larie reached across him and flicked the latch down with her beak. "That'll keep them out."

And us in, Nutley thought. He wondered whether it had been a wise decision. Especially now. With Groundling locked in with them.

At that very moment, the rest of the Grays reached the summit by the easier slope. Since they couldn't open the Box door, they began to hammer on the window. It sounded like *BANG-BANG BAM-BAM DE-BAM* as each one took a turn.

Nutley stuck his paws in his ears.

"Don't worry. That glass won't break," Larie said. "Neither will the latch. And they ain't strong enough to push the White Box down the hill."

He could barely hear her with his paws in his ears, but he heard enough. *Push the White Box down the hill?* He began to really tremble now, turned too quickly, and hit his head on the top of the Box. At that point, he fell over and rolled next to Larie's legs. His head hurt, but he didn't care. His paws and bottom hurt too, but he didn't care about them either. And his pride— well, that had been shattered long ago. Still, if the door couldn't be opened from the outside, even if the Grays managed to push the White Box down the hill, they were safe.

As long as Groundling doesn't wake up.

He thought long and hard about that. Maybe he should kill Groundling now that he was out cold. Gnaw his head off. Stomp on his tummy. Stick his tail up his nose. That's how a truly Dangerous Squirrel would act.

But Nutley didn't move. Not a hair, not an ear, not a paw. He lay next to Larie, who seemed content to have him there. Her wing tip touched his right ear. And that's when he knew, truly knew, that he wasn't the Dangerous kind of Squirrel at all.

"Here we go," Larie said.

He'd no idea what she meant, for where could they possibly go? They were locked inside the White Box.

But a moment later he understood.

When the Grays finally realized that they couldn't open the door, they leaped one after another up onto the White Box and began to bang on the top in anger.

And then there was a greater bang, as if the very Heavens had thrown down a hammer onto the Great White Box.

"Lightning," said Larie. "Sometimes the magic works."

Nutley didn't quite understand. How could he. He was inside, not outside. He couldn't see the lightning crash into a puddle where the long tail of the dryer's cord lay. He couldn't see the electricity run up the cord like a wild thing, hissing and sparking and singing out with joy, filling the cord with power. He didn't realize that with all their banging and bumping on top of the Great White Box, the Grays had pushed a button they shouldn't have pushed or pulled a knob they shouldn't have pulled.

All Nutley knew was that suddenly the round inner barrel of the Great White Box where he and Larie and the unconscious Groundling lay began to creak and groan. Then slowly it began to turn.

"Oh no!" whimpered Nutley.

"Spin Cycle!" cried Larie.

And they did indeed begin to spin—around and around and around faster and faster.

As they spun, the White Box shook and whuffled and squealed. Or maybe it was Nutley and Larie shaking, whuffling, and squealing. It was hard to tell. They went up and over, up and over dozens of times, as did Groundling, still out from his head bump, until they were all giddy and a bit sick.

The spinning went on for a long while, but at last, it slowed and then finally stopped. For some time after that, the three of them lay on the bottom of the barrel, Groundling inert and unmoving, and Larie and Nutley trying to sort themselves out.

Nutley found himself pressed against Larie's soft, feathered back. His tail was caught around her legs. Groundling lay head down by his side.

Finally, everything went quiet. Quiet inside and quiet outside as well.

"Have they gone?" whispered Nutley.

Larie unwound Nutley's tail from her legs, crept to the window, and stared out. The rain had stopped, the storm moved on, and the moon was now high overhead so all the ground around was illuminated. "I think so."

"Think so or know so?" whispered Nutley, as he clambered to his feet and joined her at the window.

Larie cocked her head to one side, listening. After a moment she said, "Know so."

"Sure?"

"Sure. And I can always fly you away from here if . . ."

"No ifs," he told her. "We have no time for ifs."

"Always good to have a plan B," she said.

He shook his head. There was no plan B. Never could have been. But he wasn't going to tell her that. "What do we do now?" he asked.

"Dead Man's Latch."

He had forgotten about that. He began to tremble.

She flipped the latch up.

And that's when he finally understood. It was not called after someone who had died but someone who *doesn't* die. Without that latch, they'd never have been able to open the door from the inside. He leaned over and pushed open the door, which creaked in protest.

Much too loud, he thought, shuddering. Everyone will be alerted.

Moonlight spilled into the White Box. Nutley realized they must have been in the Spin Cycle for a long time. The storm was over, but there were huge puddles everywhere. And bits of burned fur and sizzled tail hairs. The smell was electric.

"Help me," he said to Larie.

"Help you do what?"

"Take Groundling out of here."

"Groundling?"

"Him!" He pointed to the lump of Gray Squirrel sprawled out beside them, unmoving, and breathing uncertainly.

"Leave 'im," Larie said. "He'd have left you. Close the door and walk away."

"He'll die."

"He may already be dead," Larie said. "Or so close to it that he'd never mind."

"But if he isn't?"

"Not your problem."

But Groundling made a noise then, a soft groan.

Nutley remembered when he himself had groaned like that after being rolled down the hill. Groundling hadn't killed him then, though he could have. He'd just walked away.

I can walk away too, Nutley told himself. *But not like this.* He turned back and put his paws under Groundling's upper legs and began to haul him toward the door.

*T*his you should know:

The Red Squirrel is considered by
scientists to be a solitary animal,
shy, incapable of making friends, or
playing well with others. And that
may be so. Scientists further note
that Red Squirrels do not share food
with foreigners. So how can this
tale of Nutley and Larie be true?
Remind yourself how under certain
circumstances, a Dog and a Cat can be
best of friends, an Owl may serve as

a surrogate mother to baby Chicks,

Lately, a Tortoise and Hippo were

seen living comfortably together.

A Lioness was reported raising a

baby Oryx, though normally she

would have chased it down and eaten

it. Scientists point out that when

it is not breeding season, several

unrelated Red Squirrels may share

their quarters to keep warm in the

winter. Nature, it seems, provides

escape pods for all of us.

The Last Battle

"Oh, for silly's sake," Larie complained, as she came over to nudge the Gray Squirrel's bottom with her head. It took quite a bit of pushing and pulling, but at last, the two of them had moved Groundling to the White Box's door.

Cautiously, Nutley crawled through the open door and peered out. It was a cold night, edging toward dawn, which was only a thin red line down on the horizon.

The moon was still up, but a cloud was heading toward it. For the moment, Nutley could see perfectly and hear even better. Larie was right. The Grays *were* gone.

"All clear," he said.

"Whadda you know?" said Larie.

Nutley knew she had simply asked what Father called "Not a real question." Like *How about that?* And *What's it to you?* And *Isn't that something?*

Grabbing Groundling under the arms once again, then pulling and pulling, Nutley was finally able to leap out of the Great White Box. They landed with a thump onto something sharp and crunchy. There seemed to be a great deal of it. But now the cloud hid the moon and so he couldn't quite make out what they'd landed on.

Larie climbed out after him, standing dizzily on the ground for a moment more before gaining enough stability to fly up into the air. Her wings made a small breeze that blew Nutley's ear tufts around.

"What are you doing?" she called down to him, and this time it was a real question, for he was pulling Groundling along the crunchy path.

"I'm going to roll him down the hill," Nutley said. "Just as he did me. And if he is meant to live, he will. I can't just let him die in the White Box."

Larie hovered for a moment more before settling down onto the ground. She folded her wings and walked over to Nutley just as he reached the edge of Trash Mountain.

"I suppose you're right," she said sensibly.

"I am?" He was surprised. It was the first time she'd complimented him.

"Yes, we may need to use the White Box again as a winter home."

"Oh!" He was disappointed in her reasoning and was about to say so, when the cloud moved on and the moon shone straight down, illuminating everything. Now he could see that the crunchy things he was standing on were nuts, maybe a hundred of them, strewn around the White Box. Mostly hazelnuts but some pinecones, with pine nuts attached too. He was surprised he hadn't smelled them. But then, he'd been too busy being scared and heroic to consider food. *Whadda you know*, indeed!

Nutley was about to lean forward and pick one up, when Larie's left wing stopped him.

"What are you doing *now*?" she asked.

"About to eat some nuts. I'm starving."

"What if . . ." Larie said softly looking around, "what if it's a trap?"

Just as she spoke, the moon once more hid behind a

cloud and the top of Trash Mountain was plunged into a truly scary darkness.

"Who could gather so many nuts in such a small time and set out a trap?" Nutley whispered. But the answer was right before him. *Who indeed?* Grays climbed trees. Grays gathered nuts. Grays were devious and crafty enough to set a trap. "They couldn't have had time . . ."

"We don't know how long we were in the Box?" said Larie. "It might have been a *really* long time."

Nutley nodded and took a step back.

Suddenly, from either side, dark shadows closed in on them. Lots of dark shadows with lots of shiny eyes.

"Fly!" Nutley cried, to Larie. "Save yourself. I'll keep them busy." He gave Groundling's body a little push, rolling him over the side of the mountain. Groundling's body picked up speed at each revolution down the mountainside. Nutley could hear him saying, "Ouf!" and "Ouch!" all the way down.

So—he is alive! Nutley thought. It didn't feel as good as he'd hoped it would, but it didn't feel entirely bad either.

"SURPRISE!" about twenty slightly grating voices cried. And then one voice giggled. It sounded like a wheeze crossed with a gasp, as if the poor thing was going to die of laughter.

Behind him, there was a rustle and more laughter, this time a deeper sound. Nutley squared his shoulders and turned to face his fate.

The moon popped out again, like a Rat from a burrow. It was a dying moon, white and ghostly.

"Hush, Nawshus. Let Dada talk."

Only now Nutley realized that the shadows weren't Squirrels at all but Rats. Big Rats and small Rats and even some baby Rats. They formed two lines to one side of the White Box. Naw stepped forward. He was not as big as the biggest two Tatters, but he was certainly more composed.

"We of the Rat Community," he began, stopped, and cleared his throat. "Well, Nut-Boy . . ."

"Nutley," said Nutley and Larie together.

"We have much to thank you for."

Above there was a fluttering sound. Nutley looked up, and a delegation of Gulls appeared too.

"Ours! Ours! Ours!" they cried.

"It's about time," Larie said under her breath. "Better late than . . ."

Nutley knew that one. Mummy said it all the time when Father came home with nuts long after dark. "Than not at all." He grinned at Larie, and she grinned back. At least he *thought* she was grinning. It was hard to tell with one of the Winged Folk. After all, they have beaks, not lips. But her yellow eyes gave her away, for they were gleaming with joy.

Naw was smiling too. It did *not* improve his looks. "So we brung you something."

"All these nuts!" exclaimed Nutley, pointing.

"Well, that was an afterthought," said Nawmer, stepping forward with baby Nawshus in her arms. "Or an after-battle."

The biggest of the Tatters sidled up to her. Both his ears were ripped to shreds. His voice didn't match his body, being high and thin. "We beat them Grays up. Then we beat them down. And then we beat them off. And finally, we followed them to where the fence meets the Big Gray Road."

He must mean the Winding Road, thought Nutley, amazed that the Rats had a different name for it.

"We watched them strip the trees bare on the North Side of the road," said Nawmer. "And then I said to Dada, I said, 'Naw—that will mean nothing's left for our baby's Hero to eat for winter.'"

Naw put his arm around Nawmer, and his entire face softened, making him look almost . . .

Well, *Squirrel-like*, Nutley thought.

"I said, 'Nawmer, gal,'" and Naw began to laugh with those great descending wheezes. "I said that Squirrel is in the Great White Box and everybody knows that Thosethatgoesindon'tcomeoutagain.'" He wheezed another laugh.

Nawmer looked up at him, eyes glistening. "And I told *him* that "Everybody knows rats and gulls can't live together, but we do. Side by side. And everybody knows that Red Squirrels got no courage, begging your pardon, Nutley. But—I said—this one does."

Nutley's mouth dropped open. "Me? Courage?"

The second biggest of the Tatters gave a laugh which sounded like nuts being spit from his mouth: *ak ack ack.* "That was a wicked body slam." His paw pounded the air. *Whap! Whop!"*

"So I said, said I," Naw ended, with another great terrible wheeze, "that we had to save those nuts then and rid the North Side of those Grays. If only in memory of the Hero. Cause we thought . . ."

"You thought, but not all of us did," Nawmer told him.

"Did it!" added the two big Tatters together.

And then all the Rats shouted together, "DID IT!" And baby Nawshus leapt from his mother's arms and ran up to Nutley and hugged his leg. Hard.

The gray and white cloud of Gulls above all seemed to clear their throats at the same time. "Us! Us! Us!"

"Them, too," said Naw. "Them, too."

Nawshus held up his paws. "Up!" he said to Nutley.

And Nutley picked him up. Even though his own paws hurt. Close to, the little Rat was not exactly pretty. Rats never are. But he had a certain charm.

Larie winked at Nutley, as if she knew exactly what Nutley was thinking. She whispered, "He'll probably grow out of it."

Then pumping her wings, she flew off to join her mates.

For a moment, Nutley was sad, watching her go. But then she flew back over his head, the wind from her wings ruffling his ear tufts.

"See you tomorrow, Nut-Boy!" she called.

"Nutley," cried baby Nawshus. "It be his *name*."

This you should know:
In the real world, Red
Squirrels have been pushed
out, marginalized, by the
bigger, stronger, more
aggressive, and (some say)
smarter Grays. The Grays
carry a Squirrel pox to
which they alone are immune

but which kills the Reds. But
is there more meaning to
this little tale about Trash
Mountain than you see on
the page? Well, remember—
the word *history*, even
natural history, ends in the
word *story*. There is more
meaning here if you would
have it be so. Or at least it's
the beginning.

Afterward

Nutley made the Great White Box his *drey*, his home. It was warm in the winter, cool in the summer, and a perfect place to store his nuts. It was like a gigantic hole in a tree. Without the tree, of course.

Nawmer found him a picture of the Queen from a thrown-away magazine called *OK* which Nutley kept in memory of his Mummy. And he told all the new little Rats the stories that Mummy had told him. They especially liked the tales about Trolls. Oh, and he told them the story of the Great Battle too. They always loved that one. He taught them things his Father had said. And he and Larie remained the closest of friends thereafter, though she was the only one of the Gulls he ever got to know well.

She let him pretend to be a Flying Squirrel, though no more than once a week. He ate so well from his private stand of hazelnut trees, that he grew big and round, even in the winter, so much so that by his third year at Trash Mountain, Larie had to stop giving him rides.

As for Danger, once and only once more, because of a Fox, Nutley had to use the Dead Man's Latch to close the door. But that's another story altogether.

Really.

The Long Rive

Nutley's Trees

~ The Spur Road

Trash Mountain

Guard House

The Winding Road

Farmer Temple's Driven

The Hazelnut Trees

The 21 stones

Lazy Stream

Parts Unknown

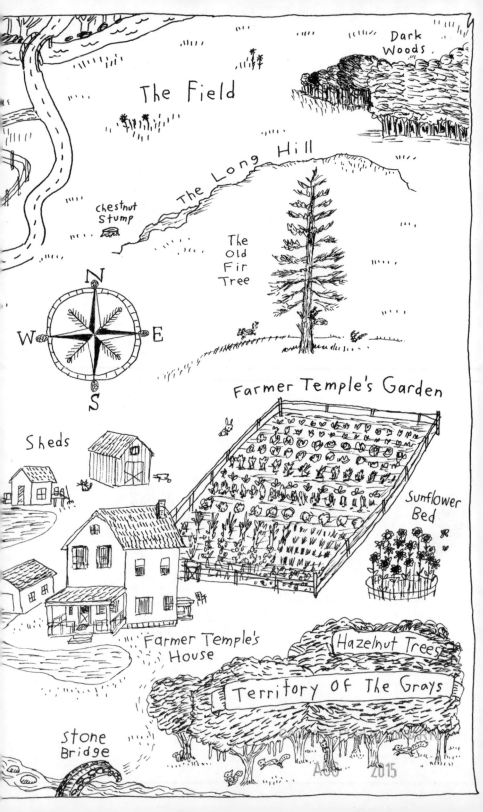